The Night Buffalo

Also by Guillermo Arriaga

Un dulce olor a muerte/The Sweet Smell of Death

Escuadrón guillotina

The
Night Buffalo

A NOVEL

Guillermo Arriaga

Translated by Alan Page

ATRIA BOOKS
New York London Toronto Sydney

ATRIA BOOKS
1230 Avenue of the Americas
New York, NY 10020

Library of Congress Cataloging Publication Data

Arriaga Jordán, Guillermo, date.
    [Búfalo de la noche. English]
    The night buffalo : a novel / Guillermo Arriaga.
        p. cm.
    I. Title.

PQ7298.1.R753B8413   2006
863'.64—dc22

                                                    2005055896

ISBN-13: 978-0-7432-8185-0
ISBN-10:   0-7432-8185-3

First Atria Books hardcover edition May 2006

10 9 8 7 6 5 4 3 2 1

ATRIA BOOKS is a trademark of Simon & Schuster, Inc.

Designed by C. Linda Dingler

Manufactured in the United States of America

For information about special discounts for bulk purchases,
please contact Simon & Schuster Special Sales at
1-800-456-6798 or business@simonandschuster.com.

For Jaime Aljure, Julio Derbez, and Eusebio Ruvalcaba

"The flashes of his eyes suddenly revealed to me that we men do not belong to one single species, but to many, and that from one species to another, within mankind, there are impassable distances, worlds irreducible to a common term, capable of producing—if from one world, one were to look into the depths of one facing him—the vertigo of the other."

—Martín Luis Guzmán

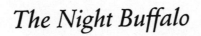

The Night Buffalo

I decided to visit Gregorio on a Saturday afternoon, three weeks after his most recent release from the hospital. It wasn't easy for me to seek him out. I thought it over for months. I was afraid of meeting him again, almost as if I were anticipating an ambush. That afternoon I walked around the block several times not daring to knock on his door. When I finally did, I was nervous, restless, and—why not say it—feeling a little cowardly.

His mother opened the door. She greeted me affectionately and then led me straight into the living room, as if she'd been awaiting my return. She called her son. Gregorio emerged on the stairs. He slowly descended the steps. He stopped and leaned on the banister. He studied my face for a few seconds, smiled, and walked toward me to give me a hug. His vehemence intimidated me and I didn't know how to respond to his gesture. I didn't know if he had really forgiven me or if we'd forgiven each other.

His mother said something meaningless and excused herself to leave us alone. We went up to Gregorio's room like we used to. We walked in and he shut the lockless door. He lay on the bed. He looked relaxed, at ease. There was nothing in his face to make me suspect he was faking it. It looked as if he'd finally regained some peace.

I sat in the usual place—the director's chair Gregorio had at his desk—and started the conversation in the stupidest and most obvious way possible:

"How do you feel?" I asked him.

Gregorio straightened up and arched his eyebrows.

"How do I look?"

"Fine."

Gregorio shrugged his shoulders.

"Well, then I'm fine."

WE SPOKE FOR HOURS, small talk. We needed to get a sense of the territory again. Especially me: I didn't want to walk back to the edge of the abyss. Out of luck, respect, or maybe just mere courtesy, he didn't ask me about Tania, even though I'm sure we both thought of her in each of our silences.

We said good-bye well into the night. We gave each other a prolonged hug. We said we'd see each other soon, for lunch or a movie. I left the house. A cold wind was trailing a vague rumor of voices and the rumble of cars along with it. It smelled of burned garbage. A streetlight flickered, intermittently lighting the sidewalk. I closed my eyes. I couldn't walk away from Gregorio. His friendship was indispensable. Even when he threatened me and hurt me, I couldn't leave him.

FOUR DAYS LATER the phone rang. I answered: mute breathing. I thought it might be a joke or one of the stupid girls who wanted to talk to my brother and were too shy to ask for him.

I was about to hang up when I heard Margarita's weak voice.

"Hello . . . Manuel?" she mumbled.

"Yeah."

"Manuel . . ." again, and was silent.

"What happened?"

"My brother . . ." she whispered. I heard her tense breathing again.

"Margarita, what happened?"

She said nothing else and hung up.

MARGARITA TRIED, but was unable to tell me the news that subsequent phone calls would confirm: Gregorio had shot himself in the head. They'd found him agonizing in a puddle of blood, with his left hand still gripping the revolver.

The boarded windows and iron bars, the lockless door, the patience, love, sedatives, shock therapy, all those months spent in mental hospitals, the pain. The pain. All useless.

Gregorio died on his mother's lap, stretched out on the backseat of the car his father feverishly drove to the hospital. He killed himself with the same gun we'd stolen years ago from a cop guarding the entrance to a convenience store. It was a rusty .38 Brazilian revolver; we'd doubted whether it worked at all until we decided to test it on a stray dog. On the first shot the mutt collapsed with its muzzle blasted to pieces. From then on until the day he died, Gregorio learned how to hide the gun in several places, avoiding the detailed searches carried out wherever he lived.

Gregorio wrapped the gun in a plastic bag—loaded with six hollow-point bullets—and buried it in a flowerpot with budding red geraniums. When we pieced the suicide together we deduced that he took the revolver out of its hiding place while pretending to tend to the plants in the garden—an activity his doctors recommended for a speedier recovery. Gregorio took the gun, hid it under his shirt, and left his work in a hurry, leaving a trowel, a spade, and a bag of fertilizer behind.

Resolute, he went up to his room. He pushed the desk against the door and entered the bathroom. He cocked the revolver, looked at himself in the mirror, held the muzzle to his left eyebrow, and pulled the trigger.

The bullet crossed diagonally through his brain, bursting through arteries, neurons, desires, tenderness, hatred, bones. Gregorio collapsed on the tiles with two holes in his skull. He was about to turn twenty-three.

JOAQUÍN, HIS YOUNGER BROTHER, took care of everything related to the burial as well as the police department's interrogations and requirements. His mother, exhausted, fell asleep on the living room sofa without even changing her bloodstained blouse. His father holed up in his son's room in search of clues to help him understand what happened. Margarita, who first focused on informing family and friends, surrendered to her impotence and fled to the house of one of her cousins, where she sank into a rocking chair, drank Diet Coke, and stared at the TV.

I went with Joaquín to the funeral home. We both chose the coffin: the cheapest and simplest one. It was all the family savings could afford, drained by Gregorio's countless medical and psychiatric expenses.

The body arrived at the funeral home at three in the morning. Luckily, a distant uncle—a somewhat prestigious lawyer—dealt with the paperwork to avoid an autopsy and to expedite the body's release from the morgue.

An employee from the funeral home asked us to go identify the body. I offered to do it: Joaquín had gone through enough.

The man led me down some stairs to a basement. Halfway there I stopped, regretting my offer. How could I face Gregorio again? Especially, how could I face him in death? Dizzy, I brought my hand to my head. I had trouble breathing. Wasn't a brief description enough? The man took me by the arm and ushered me on. In an effort to console me, he said a quick glance would be enough to finish the procedure.

We walked into a windowless room lit by tubes of fluorescent light. Gregorio, or what once was Gregorio, lay on a metal table, a white sheet drawn up to his chest. Death had given his face a light, slender expression. There were no remnants of his cold, challenging demeanor. A bandage on his left brow covered the suicidal orifice. A purplish hematoma colored his forehead. His hair, smeared with blood, looked as if it'd been slicked back with gel. His unshaven beard gave him an air of exhaustion, a kind of tedium. I stared at him for a few minutes; he looked less intimidating dead than he had alive—much less.

"It's him, right?" the man asked hesitantly upon seeing me engrossed.

I looked at Gregorio's body one last time. How to say good-bye? Say it, just like that, or squeeze him and cry beside him? How to explain to him that his death hurt and infuriated and humiliated me? How to say all this to a quiet, a stupidly quiet, corpse?

"Yes, that's Gregorio Valdés," I said, and turned to leave.

THE WAKE WAS sparsely attended. Even once the news spread, few dared to give their condolences: The body of a suicide is always upsetting.

Gregorio's family wandered aimlessly through the chapel.

His mother napped with her grief in isolated corners. His father digressed in the middle of his sentences, leaving them unfinished and sunk in exasperating silences. Margarita babbled nonsense and Joaquín, swollen with fatigue, clumsily tried to stay awake.

The parents endured everything: gossip, furtive glances, fake mourning. Though atheists, they allowed a priest (for whose services the funeral home opportunely charged under the pretext of a donation) to conduct mass. They even allowed in a cheap tabloid reporter who spent his time shamelessly snooping around.

AT FIVE O'CLOCK in the afternoon, the funeral cortege set out. Only four cars followed the hearse to the graveyard. Thanks to a dispensation obtained by the lawyer uncle, Gregorio was cremated. I shuddered while watching the blue smoke surging from the crematory's chimney. Even in the small amphitheater I'd still felt Gregorio close to me: palpable, human. Now the smoke spirals signaled his definitive death.

I didn't wait for them the deliver the urn. Crying, I snuck out a side door to the cemetery. Since I didn't have any money for a taxi or a bus, I decided to go home on foot. I walked down the streets without noticing the countless stalls of street vendors, the tumult outside the metro station, the traffic, the car exhaust—sometimes also blue.

I arrived home. My parents were waiting for me, worried about my being late. They'd only quickly stopped by the funeral home. They couldn't even take five minutes of the hopeless atmosphere.

We ate dinner in silence. When we finished my mother took

my hand and kissed my forehead. I noticed her eyes were swollen.

I went up to my room. I grabbed the phone and called Tania. Her sister told me she was already asleep. Moody, she asked me if I wanted her to wake Tania up. I said no, that I'd call her later.

Tania neither wanted to go to the wake nor the cremation. For her, Gregorio wasn't dead just yet. She'd told me in the morning.

"He's still plotting something," she assured me. "Gregorio won't leave just like that."

She sounded anxious, agitated. I scolded her for being so childishly afraid of him.

"Don't forget he was the King Midas of destruction," she pronounced.

"Was," I pointed out.

"He always will be."

She said it wasn't a coincidence that Gregorio had committed suicide a few days after seeing me, or that he'd specifically chosen the twenty-second of February to blow his brains out.

"It's his way of getting his own, can't you see? The son of a bitch is smearing his blood on us."

I wasn't able to calm her down, much less convince her to come with me to the wake or burial. Her attitude seemed petty and unfair; the dead don't deserve to be left alone.

I TRIED TO READ for a while but couldn't concentrate. I turned off the light and lay down. Exhausted, I soon fell asleep. At midnight, I woke up with the feeling that an earwig had sprung from Gregorio's lifeless mouth and jumped on me to bury itself in one of my forearms. I leapt out of bed and rubbed my body desperately till I finally calmed down. I dreamt of an earwig again. I'd dreamt of earwigs dozens of times.

Sweating, I walked toward the window and opened it. The wind brought the night's breath: wailing sirens, barking, music in the distance. The cold air refreshed me. I went back to my bed and sat on the edge of the mattress. I remembered the body on the metal table. Gregorio had always wanted to murder someone, to touch the limits of death. Now he'd done it.

I turned on the bedside lamp. From the nightstand, I grabbed the frame with Tania's photograph in it. Dressed in a high school uniform, Tania looked at the camera smiling, her hair falling over her shoulders in layers. "I love you Manuel" was written in one of the corners of the portrait. Underneath was her signature and a blurred date: February twenty-second. Why did loving her have to hurt so much?

I put the picture back in its place and turned on the TV with the hope that some insipid nighttime programming would lull me to sleep.

I GOT UP AT DAWN, ragged from insomnia. I went down to the kitchen and poured myself a glass of milk. No one else was awake yet. I started reading the previous day's newspaper and found nothing interesting. I left the paper on the table and half-heartedly drank the milk. Six in the morning and I couldn't find anything to do.

I decided to take a shower. As I undressed, I looked at the tiles. They were of a similar color and texture to the ones in Gregorio's bathroom. I saw him falling backward with his skull burst open. I could clearly hear the snap of his body bouncing off the towel rack, the bubbling of his blood, his hoarse panting.

I turned on the shower and stuck my head under the freezing stream until the nape of my neck hurt. I abruptly pulled my head out. Hundreds of cold drops slid down my back. I sat on the floor and shivered. I grabbed a towel and wrapped myself in it, but I couldn't stop shaking for a long while.

I left the bathroom and lay down on the bed naked, with my hair still soaking wet. I closed my eyes and fell asleep.

I WOKE UP FOUR HOURS LATER, numb: I'd forgotten to close the window and the wind was circulating through the room. Without entirely waking up, I sat up to close it. I could hear the bustle of children playing in a nearby school and a song from a woman pinning up clothes on a neighboring rooftop. I spotted a note on the floor that my mother had slid under the door. Tania and Margarita had called.

I tried reaching Tania first, but no one answered at her house. I remembered it was Thursday and thought she and her sister were probably at school. I looked at the clock: twelve-thirty. In fifteen minutes, Tania would walk out of her Textile Design class and go have a cup of coffee and play dominoes with her friends. It pissed me off that Tania would go on with her daily life, as if the bullet that tore through that Tuesday afternoon weren't reason enough to stop it dead.

Then I dialed Gregorio's house (was it still his house? A dead man's house?). Margarita answered. She explained that her parents weren't there but that her mother had asked her to invite me to dinner.

"What for?" I asked.

"Well, to chat, I think," she answered, disconcerted.

I refused without even considering the possibility.

"I can't tonight."

She insisted, but I still declined. She remained silent for a few seconds.

"Can you come right now?" she inquired nervously.

"What for?"

Margarita sighed deeply.

"I need to see you," she said under her breath.

Her request seemed out of place. Margarita and I had had a fleeting, secret, purely sexual relationship, of which we soon got tired. We decided never to discuss it again and swore never to tell anyone.

"You don't need to see me," I said aggressively.

"It's not for what you're thinking," she snapped back angrily, "it's for something completely different."

"Oh yeah?"

"You're an asshole."

Margarita grew silent.

"I'm sorry," I said.

She kept quiet for a few more seconds, clicked her tongue, and started muttering.

"About a month ago . . . or three weeks . . . I can't remember, Gregorio asked me to keep a box for him . . . a small box . . . of chocolates . . ."

She stopped, gulped, and continued.

"He asked me to keep it safe and now . . ."

Her voice cracked, but she didn't cry.

"I can't find it, Manuel," she went on. "I can't find the fucking box."

"Where did you leave it? Think."

No, she couldn't remember. She couldn't even remember that she was the first one to walk into the bathroom after the shot, that she found her older brother gushing blood next to the sink, that she tried to stop the bleeding by stuffing the wounds with pieces of toilet paper, that she carried the limp body all the way to the car, and that she was left standing in the middle of the street without knowing what to do. No, Margarita couldn't remember anything.

"Help me look for it," she implored, "please."

I agreed to meet her at her house at seven o'clock that night, before her parents returned. I promised her that together we'd find the box, that she shouldn't worry. She sighed a good-bye and hung up. I wanted to kiss her again, to stroke her and make love to her.

I GOT UP OUT OF BED. My head and neck ached. I walked toward the closet. For a long time, I stared at my clothes, indecisive about what to wear. I decided to put on some jeans, sneakers, and a black T-shirt. It had been awhile since I'd worn T-shirts. I hadn't worn Polo shirts or short-sleeve shirts either. I wanted to avoid people noticing the scars on my left biceps. They were unpleasant, reddish marks left over from when I rubbed my arm with a pumice stone. I'd tried to erase a tattoo I'd gotten with Gregorio on an April night in a neighborhood near El Chopo.

He insisted that we have the silhouette of an American buffalo tattooed on our left arms. Gregorio even asked for us to be tattooed with the same needles, so that the ink would mark us mixed with our blood.

At first I didn't mind, but after a few months the buffalo became an increasingly intolerable symbol. To look at my left biceps eventually infuriated me: I'd fallen into another trap set by Gregorio in his obsession.

The tattoo meant a pact of blind loyalty between us. But how could I talk of loyalty when, back then, I was sleeping with Tania on a daily basis? What loyalty could I profess to a guy who spent most of the year locked away in mental hospitals? What fucking loyalty?

Gregorio, however, demanded that loyalty, minute by minute, even when he knew it was false. And he demanded it through cheating, blackmail, threats.

Gregorio slowly, stealthily fenced me in. Bit by bit he started to control every one of my daily movements. His presence, even at a distance, surrounded, subdued me. Too late, I realized that the reason for the tattoo was to consolidate his siege, to stalk me in and from my body.

That's why, after rubbing myself raw with the pumice stone, I scraped the live flesh with a kitchen knife. I tried to remove even the last hint of ink from my tissues, without caring if I was crisscrossing my biceps with deep and desperate slices.

That afternoon, my arm ended up swollen and bleeding. I had to go to a clinic, where a doctor sewed up three of the wounds. One of them needed eight stitches.

I had antitetanus shots and high doses of penicillin injected into me. It took some time to heal and when the scabs fell off it looked like a claw mark with glossy edges. Even though I tore up my arm, I was unsuccessful: The diffuse lines of the blue buffalo are still visible.

From then on I tried to hide my scars. Not out of vanity, but because people have an annoying habit of asking about the origins of scars and I was no longer in the mood to explain mine.

That Thursday I put on the black T-shirt, not to challenge curious glances, but to remember that the past, no matter how much one may pretend, is impossible to tear out, that it remains like an old burn mark that flares up again and again, and that it's better to live with it than against it.

I WENT DOWN to the kitchen and saw Marta, the woman who helped do the ironing. She told me that my mother had gone to the market in my brother's car and that she'd left hers in case I needed anything.

I left hoping to find Tania at the university. I hadn't seen her in three days. Halfway there I realized that I'd left without anything warm to wear, and nothing to hide my scars.

I arrived at two in the afternoon. There were few people at the university at that time. I went looking for Tania's classroom: B-112. I looked through the window in the door and didn't see her. I signaled one of her friends to come out of the classroom. When I asked her about Tania she said that she hadn't shown up since the previous day.

I called Tania's house from a pay phone, but no one answered. Disconcerted, I wandered down the university's empty hallways. I thought of where I might find her. When she was depressed or wanted to be alone, she liked to go to the zoo to watch the jaguars. She also used to go to the airport. She'd sit at one of the café tables, next to the large windows angled toward the runways, and watch the planes endlessly taking off and landing. She never told me why she went to these places when she needed to find peace.

I FELT I'D FIND TANIA at the zoo and headed over there via Paseo de la Reforma. The three o'clock traffic moved slowly. A slight accident between a taxi driver and a woman driving a minivan packed with little girls had aggravated the gridlock. They had blocked two lanes. The woman's hands flailed, almost touching the taxi driver's face, while he just watched her with a smirk. From inside the van, the girls, dressed in brown Catholic school uniforms, stared at the scene, frightened. What did Tania read in the jaguar's spots?

It took me fifty minutes to get there. To top it off, I parked the car twenty blocks away. I walked toward the zoo down a path that ran through Chapultepec park. The wind blew, carrying dry leaves and trash. I regretted not having brought a sweater or jacket.

When I arrived at the entrance to the zoo, groups of secondary school students were filing out. One of them walked with his hands in his pockets, staring at the ground, detached from his classmates' shoving and joking. He reminded me of Gregorio at that age.

I went straight to the jaguar pit but didn't find Tania.

I stayed awhile to watch them. The enormous male slept under a tree, while the female, smaller, took shelter from the wind between the rocks. For several minutes they didn't move, then the male got up, raised his head and stretched, and lazily sauntered toward the female. He sniffed her, growled tamely at her, and flopped down beside her. That was it.

DISHEARTENED, I decided to leave. The wind increased, a few of the blasts forming whirls of dust and straw. Other people were also hurrying to leave the grounds. A man bumped into me and mumbled a "sorry" without stopping. I crossed my arms to guard myself against the growing cold.

Out of the corner of my right eye, as I hurried, I spotted an animal pacing vigorously inside its cage. I walked over to take a look. It was a large coyote, with a thick pelt layered with shades of gold and ochre. The canine paced back and forth, tracing imaginary circles. Its vivacity, its nerve, contrasted with the felines' indolence.

The sky darkened and thick drops started to fall. Stragglers were running to take cover from the imminent storm. Suddenly, a gale cracked the branch of a nearby tree. The crunch made the coyote stop. He turned toward the tree as if to verify the source of the disaster. He then swiveled his head, crossed his yellow gaze with mine, and watched me fixedly.

A few seconds later, he continued his circular trotting. I walked away little by little, without taking my eyes off him, convinced that behind those bars, life pulsed in its purest essence.

BY THE TIME I left the zoo it was raining torrentially. Soaked, I got into the car, my socks and sneakers covered in mud. My hands were numb and, shaking, I left for Margarita's house.

I got there half an hour later. The rain had let up and was now only barely drizzling. I got out of the car still dripping and rang the doorbell several times. Margarita didn't answer. I threw some pebbles at her window to announce my arrival, like I used to. A light went on and a shadow appeared in the window. Margarita leaned out and signaled for me to wait.

She opened the door looking broken.

"I'm sorry," she said as she let me in, "I didn't realize I fell asleep."

I wiped the soles of my sneakers on the welcome mat and left a mess. Margarita smiled.

"Don't worry," she said.

She leaned over and greeted me with a kiss on the cheek. As she did, her lips touched a drop of water that trickled down my cheek. She took two steps back and looked me over.

"You're soaked, you're going to get sick."

Without saying a word she left me in the hallway and walked up the stairs. She came back with a towel and a change of clothes. She held out her arms to hand them over, but thinking that the clothes might be Gregorio's, I didn't dare take them.

"They're Joaquín's," she explained when she saw me waver.

I took them and headed to the guest bathroom. Margarita stopped me.

"You can change here," she said, "my parents said they'd be back by eight-thirty and Joaquín is with them."

I stood there, confused, without knowing what to do. On that spot, on that very rug, we'd made love. We fucked slithering between the furniture, in the dark, without talking, almost without wanting to touch each other. We did it one night when her parents had to run off to the mental hospital on an emergency—in one of his fits, Gregorio had amputated two of his right toes with a shard of glass and put them in his mouth, threatening to swallow them and mutilate another part of his body if any nurse or doctor dare come near him.

Margarita looked me in the eyes. She started a phrase with "Manuel, I . . ." but she left it unfinished. She smiled languidly and stroked the scar on my arm.

"Does it hurt?" she asked innocently.

"No, scars don't hurt." I lied: that scar would never stop hurting.

She smiled again, now much more sadly. She asked me for the towel; I turned my back toward her and she started to dry my hair in soft movements. I felt her breath on the nape of my neck.

"You smell like ivy," she said.

"What?"

"Yes, ivy," she repeated. "Like the ivy we have on the garden wall, that's what it smells like when we water it."

Just like that, she started to talk about the ivy, the silver threads the snails left as they dragged themselves across the branches, the noise the lizards made as they scampered away to hide inside the leaves, the cat that used to walk across the fence in the evenings, the calla lilies Joaquín broke with his football as a boy.

She talked and talked about a world that seemed to center on the garden—a world without pain, without wrath, without gunshots in the middle of the afternoon. I turned around to face her. I grabbed her by the wrists and pulled her toward me. Margarita let the towel fall. She smiled, squeezing her lips.

"Hey, you're freezing. I hope you don't get pneumonia," she said.

I kissed her on the knuckles and let her go. I picked the towel up from the floor and went to the guest bathroom. She stretched her arm out to try to stop me, but she seemed to regret it and pulled it away automatically.

I WALKED INTO the bathroom and locked the door. I always did: I couldn't stand the notion that someone could burst in on my privacy. I turned on the hot water and let the sink fill to the brim. Then I put my hands in and held them there until the numbness wore off.

The phone rang. Margarita answered after the eighth ring. I listened to her gradually lower her voice. I pricked up my ear but she ended up speaking in almost inaudible whispers and I no longer paid attention.

I got naked, dipped the towel in the hot water, and rubbed my body until I warmed up. I wiped the fog off the mirror and looked at my face. It seemed foreign to me, entirely foreign.

I plunged my face into the water in the basin. I held my breath as long as possible and then slowly let the air out. The bubbling relaxed me. I wanted to sleep under the water. I leaned my forehead against the bottom of the basin and closed my eyes. My head swayed in the warm current. I remained like this for awhile until I heard some distant, metallic knocking on the door. I pulled out the plug and, without moving my head, waited for the water to drain. The sink emptied and I could clearly hear Margarita's voice offering me coffee.

"No thanks," I answered.

I heard her walk away toward the kitchen. I raised my eyes and looked at myself in the mirror again. My face still seemed foreign.

I WALKED OUT of the bathroom and found Margarita sitting on one of the living room sofas (the same one her mother slept on for hours after her son killed himself). The room was dark, only lit by the light from the stairwell.

"I made you some lemon tea," she said and pointed to a steaming mug on the glass coffee table.

I took the tea and started to drink it in short slurps. It was a little sweet. I sat next to Margarita. She grabbed my hand and squeezed it.

"I feel as if I'm falling and if I don't grab on to something I'm going to crash," she said.

She let go of my hand and stared at the chimney. Her arm was barely touching mine. I could feel her warm skin, her soft hair's imperceptible caress. Would it have been worth trying to love her at some point? Because despite having penetrated her dozens of times, despite having licked her from top to toe, despite kissing her breathlessly, she was never closer to me than with that brush of arms.

Suddenly, Margarita stood up.

"Your clothes, where did you leave them?" she asked anxiously.

"In the bathroom."

"I'll be right back, I'm going to put them in the dryer."

She left, diligently, as if drying my clothes were a task that could not wait. I went into the laundry room and found her cross-legged on the floor, absorbed, watching the clothes spin in the dryer. She asked me to turn off the light.

"What's the matter?" I asked.

"Nothing."

In the darkness, the machine's whirring sounded even stronger. Filtering through a half-open shutter, a draught of wind made a hanging bedsheet billow at one end of the room. Flashes of a street lamp reflected off a bowl full of water.

Something, probably a metal button on the pants, started knocking against the dryer's window, making a monotonous, irritating rattle. Margarita got up, turned a knob and stopped the machine. She pulled out the clothes, bundled them up and started the dryer again.

"They'll be ready in five minutes," she said and remained pensive for a moment. She looked at me and breathed deeply.

"I never told you," she mumbled, "but I didn't get my period for a month and a half. I was sure I was pregnant."

"Whose was it?" I asked clumsily.

She looked at me harshly.

"Who the fuck d'you think?"

She buried her chin in her chest, bit her lips, and went on without taking her eyes off the floor.

"I didn't know what to do, I was afraid to buy one of those home pregnancy tests."

She sighed and was silent. She raised her face, brushed her hair back and went on.

"I was scared, I had no idea what was going to happen or who could help me. And I didn't know how to tell you because, Manuel, I was terrified of you. . . . Can you believe it?"

She was quiet again. Pensive, she swept her eyes over the room and smiled a sadder and sadder smile.

"Back then I used to come right here, and with the slightest excuse, I'd start the washer or dryer and listen: slosh, slosh. You're going to think I'm a little crazy, but when I listened to them I didn't feel alone. . . . Hidden away in this room for hours and hours, I'd put my hands on my belly trying to figure out whether something was moving inside me."

Again, she mumbled "inside me" and grew quiet. Her eyes were lost in the emptiness, in the memory of a being that never was there. The dryer stopped and Margarita asked me to turn on the light. She opened the door and touched the clothes repeatedly.

"They're ready," she confirmed.

She grabbed the bundle and held it to her cheek.

"They're warm, look," she said and held the clothes over my face. "Feel it?"

Margarita's eyes lit up. I drew close to her and kissed her softly on the lips. She reacted by giving me a slight bump on the chest. She smiled, this time without sadness.

"You should change while the clothes are still warm," she said, then squeezed my arm and left.

As I watched her leave I realized I'd never seen her cry.

WE LOOKED FOR Gregorio's box in the kitchen, living room, and study, finding nothing. We even checked the pantry shelves, the guest room closet, her father's desk drawers, the medicine cabinet, and the storage closet under the stairs. Nothing.

Margarita suggested we search upstairs. We went up and as I walked past Gregorio's room, I felt vertigo. Just two days earlier, Gregorio had gone through the door dripping blood, staining the hardwood floor of the corridor, the stairs, the entrance hallway, the street, the car seats, his mother's dress, his father's hands.

I couldn't resist the possibility of finding a single drop of his blood (Who cleaned them? Who scrubbed them with soap and water?). I wanted to leave, to run away as soon as possible from that bloodstained house, from those parents who wanted to have dinner with me and who were unable to avoid the gunshot that destroyed their son's skull, from Margarita who watched me with her melancholy smile and who I didn't know if I could ever love. I wanted to run from Gregorio and his blood.

I thought Margarita would ask me what was wrong as soon as she saw me leaning against the wall, or that she would make some caustic remark about my pasty skin. She just took my hand and pulled me into her parent's bedroom.

"I think I know where the box might be," she muttered.

We walked in and she headed determinedly toward the walk-in closet. She looked through the shelves, opened several boxes and shook her head.

"It's not here either. Fuck!"

She started to despair. We went to her room. She walked into the closet and turned it inside out, messing up blouses, shoes, skirts. She pulled out the drawers and emptied them one by one. The floor was covered in a mess of notebooks, beauty products, and underwear. She then bent down to feel under the bed.

"Forget it," I said.

She turned to look at me, indignant.

"I can't, I can't, don't you get it?" she snapped back.

She kept on pulling out clothes. I asked her if she knew what was in the box.

"No," she answered.

WE FOUND IT when Margarita broke a bottle of perfume that spilled on some books stacked up next to the dressing table. The box was among them, and looked like an encyclopedia volume from the side. Margarita knelt down and picked it up by the edges. She inspected it and cleaned the perfume with a sweater. The room was impregnated with a spiky smell of roses.

"I never would've found it there," she said with a half smile.

She gave me the box. As I took it, a small shard of glass got stuck in my left thumb. I pushed it out with my fingernail. The splinter jumped and a drop of blood fell on the box's cover. It expanded on the cardboard, as if it were another cherry like the ones pictured. A fourth cherry: redder, more real.

Margarita stood up and opened the window to ventilate the room. The wind came in, shaking the curtain. It was raining outside.

"Isn't the smell annoying?"

I nodded. She picked up the books, taking care not to cut herself, and set them down along the windowsill.

"They're going to get wet," I warned.

Margarita put her hand over them and held it there for a few seconds.

"I don't think so; the rain is slanting the other way."

She turned around, studied the floor, and lifted up a handkerchief. She walked toward the dressing table and bent over to pick up the pieces of broken glass. She took the larger fragments and put them on the cloth. When I tried to help her she pushed me aside.

"Stop, you'll get another splinter."

"You might, too."

"Yeah, but I broke it."

I moved away. Margarita stood up, shook the handkerchief over the wastebasket, and threw it on the floor again.

"I'll vacuum the rest tomorrow," she said.

She walked over to the door and turned off the light.

"Let's get out of here. The smell is making me dizzy."

I caught up with her and held her by the shoulder. She turned to look at me. The hallway was dark.

"What would you have done if you really were pregnant?"

"I don't know, I don't know . . ."

She raised her face and stared at me fixedly.

"What about you?" she inquired.

"I'd turn on the washing machine, the dryer, the stove, the microwave, the toaster, the TV . . ."

She smiled and stroked my cheek.

"You didn't shave today, did you?"

I took her hand and kissed it.

"I like it when you're scratchy," she said sweetly.

She moved her hand back and sighed. Slowly, she looked away.

"I would've had an abortion," she mumbled pensively. She turned around and disappeared down the stairwell's dark gap.

WE SAT IN the living room. In my hands, the box seemed to be much larger and heavier than it really was. One of those things we try to get rid of as soon as possible. Margarita asked me not to open it. She was afraid to. Once, Gregorio had asked her to keep a box just like this for him. Margarita put it in her closet and, in a few days, it started to stink. As soon as she opened it, she found the rotten tatters of some animal's intestine and a dozen earwigs scurrying to hide among the guts.

It turned out the innards belonged to one of the neighbors' cats, which Gregorio had mashed to a pulp with a rock and half-buried under a hedge in the garden. Regarding the earwigs, Gregorio claimed they had emerged from his mouth while he slept, that they were of his own flesh and blood, and that he'd found no better way to keep them alive.

With a knife, I cut the strips of tape that sealed the box. Margarita withdrew, mistrustful. I opened it, somewhat ill at ease. There were no surprises: several pieces of paper were arranged into four packets tied with colored ribbons: letters, notes on napkins, medical prescriptions. Some pictures were in an attached envelope. I called Margarita, who'd hidden in the kitchen. She approached warily.

"What's inside?"

I pulled out one of the packages and showed it to her.

"This: letters, photographs."

Despite my insistence, she refused to look at them. She asked me to take them home and look through them there.

"If there's nothing bad about them," she said, "give them back to me; if there is, burn them."

24

• • •

I AGREED TO TAKE the box to my car so her parents wouldn't see it. Margarita supposed that it must have held something that could hurt them. Apparently, none of Gregorio's actions, dead or alive, was harmless.

I went out into the street protected by an umbrella. The rain fell thick. Large quantities of water flowed down the gutters and huge puddles flooded the street. Margarita had to lend me two plastic bags to tie around my sneakers so my feet wouldn't get soaked.

I jumped over the gutter, tripped, and as I tried to regain my balance, the box slipped from my hands and fell on the wet pavement. I quickly picked it up and dried it by dragging it over my pants. I held it tightly and, sidestepping several puddles, reached my car on the opposite side of the street. I took out the keys and hurriedly opened the door, throwing the box on the backseat. I pulled in the umbrella as best I could and closed the door.

I stretched out in the driver's seat. The roof rumbled with the falling rain and rushes of water streamed down the windshield. I wiped the foggy window and looked at Gregorio's house. Water was dripping everywhere. Water and more water. Through the torrential rain I could make out the blurry figure of Margarita looking out the door. I saw she was trying to point at something. I lowered the window to try to see her more clearly, but the rain forced me to roll it up again.

I turned on the inside light and opened the box. The bottom was soaked, but none of the papers were damp. I looked at the four packets tied with the colored ribbons. Gregorio hadn't given these to Margarita innocently. There was a purpose, a message. I asked myself if it was worth following the game till the end. I was tempted to tear up every piece of paper, every photograph, and throw them into the river that ran into the gutter. It could be the moment to finish with Gregorio, to let him truly die.

I put the packets back into place, closed the box, and turned off the light. I gripped the umbrella, got out of the car, and walked out into a curtain of water. Again, I got soaked and was cold.

I asked Margarita what she had tried to signal to me.

"Nothing," she answered.

MARGARITA'S PARENTS got home around ten, claiming it was due to the heavy traffic caused by the rain. They'd gone to visit some relatives and then to pay off the debt to the funeral home with borrowed money. Joaquín said hello and went up to his room for the night. Regardless, his mother set six places. This included one at the right-hand head of the table, where Gregorio usually sat.

No dinner had been prepared. The mother apologized to me and emptied out two roasted chickens onto some plates next to a half-open bag of potato chips. The chicken was cold and the chips soggy and bland.

We sat at the table, solemn and silent. The father said that it gave him great pleasure that I should join them, that he considered me part of the family and that it was good to have me at their side at that moment.

We ate in silence. I served myself a drumstick and ate only half of it. The mother forgot to offer me something to drink. Despite my thirst I didn't dare bother her. Engrossed, she turned circles with her fork without bringing the meat to her mouth.

Once we were finished with dinner, the father opened a bottle of Chilean wine. He poured it into water glasses, half-gestured a toast, and drank with his eyes closed. No one drank with him.

Margarita brought coffee. Though I dislike it, I decided to have some. I wanted to warm up and relax a little. The coffee turned out to be the best part of dinner.

Near midnight, the phone rang. Startled, the mother got up to answer it in the kitchen. She came back looking distraught.

"It's Tania's mom. She says her daughter left for school at seven AM and they haven't heard from her since. She's asking if anyone knows where she might be."

We all shook our heads. A deeper, more uncomfortable silence. Tania was the only woman Gregorio had ever loved. Now Tania was the woman I loved.

Margarita made a silly remark that helped ease the tension. The father celebrated it exaggeratedly and took advantage of the occasion to serve himself a fifth glass of wine. Then he grew silent and drank with his eyes closed again.

The phone call left me uneasy. Two years ago Tania had disappeared for a week. The police were notified on the second day. First they thought she might have been kidnapped; then, an accident or even murder. I can still remember the anxious nights as we combed the morgues and hospitals.

Just like that, Tania had returned, dirty and gaunt. She didn't say a word about her disappearance—not to me, not to her parents. Everything was an enigma she refused to reveal. She must have felt a little bit guilty, because from then on she made sure her parents knew where she was going, who she was going with, and how she could be reached. Only in her occasional depressions would she go to the zoo or the airport, and she would only stay for three or four hours.

. . .

NERVOUS, I asked to borrow the phone. I went into the kitchen and dialed home. My brother Luis answered half-asleep.

"What's the matter?" he asked, annoyed.

"Did anyone call me?"

"I don't know, why the fuck do you need to know at this hour of the night?"

"It's urgent."

"I'll tell you tomorrow."

"Please."

"Hang on," he mumbled angrily.

He dropped the phone on the floor and I heard his steps walking away. Margarita walked into the kitchen and stood next to me. She took my hand and squeezed it. I let go of her when I heard her mother approaching.

After a few minutes, Luis picked up the receiver again.

"Mom says Tania called you at five."

"What else?"

"Nothing else."

"She didn't say where she was?"

Luis gave me a categorical "no" and hung up. I had a throbbing in my temple, a bad feeling about this.

I left the kitchen ready to go. I said good-bye and thanked them for dinner. The mother came up to me and hugged me limply, as if she were drunk. She leaned her head on my chest and repeated several times: "Thank you for coming, thank you for coming." Under the fabric of her dress I felt her skinny body and its jutting bones; a body in the process of drying up.

She pulled away from me, then kissed me on the cheek.

"Drive safely, sweetie," she mumbled and kissed me again, "and I hope Tania's okay."

The father squeezed my hand when I said good-bye. When he noticed I didn't have anything to cover myself with, he went into his study for a jacket. It was a good jacket, stuffed with goose down. Exactly what I needed. I tried to turn it down, but he insisted and helped me put it on. I promised I'd give it back as soon as possible.

MARGARITA WALKED me to the car. The rain had stopped. I could hear the murmur of water trickling toward the drain. The outlines of the houses blurred in the mist. I opened the car door; Margarita, behind me, remained silent. I turned to say good-bye. "See you," I said and kissed her slightly on the lips. I spun to get into the car and she grabbed me by the arm.

"What's the matter?" I asked.

She stared at me without answering and clicked her tongue. She looked worried. In what was more a fraternal than loving gesture, I took her by the shoulders and drew her toward me.

"Tell me what's wrong."

Without taking her eyes off me, she brought her hand to her forehead and brushed a strand of hair away from her face.

"Before, when you were changing in the bathroom, the phone rang," she said, paused for a long time, watched a gray cat cross the street, then turned her eyes toward me again.

"It was Tania."

I pulled away from her and moved her aside.

"Why didn't you tell me?"

She looked at the cat again, which had now hidden under a tree. She hissed to scare it away. The cat left its hiding place and examined us. Then it trotted a few steps and in two jumps climbed a fence and disappeared.

"Why didn't you tell me?" I repeated.

With her eyes still fixed on where the cat had disappeared, Margarita shrugged her shoulders.

"I don't know."

Her attitude started to irritate me. I planted myself squarely in front of her. She changed posture and started to watch the water running into the sewer.

"Why do you keep playing these games?" I scolded her.

"I'm not playing games," she answered, annoyed.

I found it hard to understand her evasions. She wasn't doing it out of jealousy, I was sure of that. If anyone had helped to cover up my relationship with Tania, she had.

"So?" I inquired.

She remained pensive, without answering. Tired of her secrecy, I let myself drop onto the seat and turned the motor on without closing the door.

"I really don't know what you're playing at."

Margarita ducked until her face was level with mine.

"I'm not the one playing, Manuel, it's Tania."

I shut the engine off.

"What do you mean?"

"She's the one who asked me not to tell you anything."

"Why?"

"The only thing I can tell you is that she's okay, so you can relax."

She finished, turned around, and started to walk back in without missing a beat. I got out of the car and caught up to her.

"Margarita, what's going on?"

Something seemed to bother her. She raised her hands as if to better explain herself but remained silent.

"Nothing, nothing's the matter," she mumbled.

"Why are you acting like this?"

The wind picked up. Margarita wrapped her arms around herself to take cover from the cold.

"The air is freezing," she murmured.

She raised her head to feel where the wind was coming from, and her hair blew over her face. She brusquely pulled it away.

"Can I ask you a question?" she said.

I nodded.

"Did you tell Tania anything about us?"

The question surprised me. The pact was clear: never to reveal our secret.

"No. Especially her. Why?"

"No reason," she answered, just when it seemed as if she was about to say something else.

She breathed in deeply and when she exhaled, her breath formed a small cloud.

"I'd better go," she said, conflicted. "I'm freezing."

She kissed me and quickly pulled away.

I turned on the car and let it warm up for a while. I felt confused and exhausted. I put the car in gear and just as I was about to leave Margarita knocked on the window.

"What's the matter?" I asked as I lowered the glass.

Margarita put both hands on the door, leaned in and faced me.

"Tania said she'd be in 803," she said in a low voice.

We looked at each other for a moment. Margarita abruptly pulled her hands off the door and walked away, resolute, without looking back.

• • •

I TRIED TO FEND off sleep as I drove. It was past one in the morning and I'd slept badly for the previous couple of nights. I desperately wanted to close my eyes and keep them shut for two weeks, a month, a year. I wanted to forget who I was and what I was doing driving a car, chasing the woman I loved down the streets of a city overflowing with rainwater.

Surely Margarita didn't know what 803 meant. It wasn't a code, it was a specific number of a specific place: a room in a city motel. Room 803 was our place, and by saying "our" I don't just mean Tania, but also, even though it pains me to admit it, Gregorio Valdés.

I drove to the motel and parked in front of the reception area. The curtains were closed in only two of the driveways. There was no car in 803.

The rooms had two doors, one leading to the driveway and another onto the patio. I knocked on the patio door several times but no one opened. A young employee—tall, strong, with curly hair, who I didn't know, asked me what I wanted.

"To get inside," I answered.

"It's occupied," he said flatly.

"I know."

Another man, dark and short, who I also didn't know, joined the first.

"You can't bother the clients," he said, displeased.

"I don't want to bother anyone, I just want in."

"That's not going to happen."

"Why don't you just lend me the key?"

The dark-skinned man took this as a provocation and, snapping his fingers, ordered:

"Get the fuck out now, you son of a bitch."

He opened his jacket and the butt of a revolver shone from

his waist. On some other occasion this would have been the perfect excuse to lay into him, but the last thing I wanted was trouble. I was too tired.

"What time did Pancho get off work?" I asked.

My question threw them both off.

"You know him?"

"Yeah, him and Mr. Camariña."

Upon hearing the name of the motel owner, the man with the gun relaxed his defiant attitude and zipped up his jacket.

"I'm the guy who's paying for this room," I clarified, even though Tania was really the one who paid for it.

They both apologized, noting they were new at the job. I asked them about Tania and they said she'd left about half an hour ago.

"She left without saying anything," said the man.

The curtain on one of the driveways half-opened. A thin man, with the look of a bureaucrat, appeared. He looked at us mistrustfully and got into a run-down Dodge Dart. The woman accompanying him ducked in her seat so we wouldn't see her. The car moved forward and the employees immediately looked away as I watched the couple drive past us, forgetting that the basic rule in any motel is never to look directly at other people.

THE CURLY-HAIRED employee brought the key, unlocked the door, and opened it.

"If you need anything else, let us know," he said, eyeing me.

I walked in and turned on the light. There was the usual room: the usual bed, the nightstand, the lamp, the mirror, the painting, the dresser.

Tania had been there. The covers were wrinkled and one of

the pillows had been stacked on top of the other one. A book—
Músico de Cortesanas by Eusebio Ruvalcaba—lay open on top of
the dresser.

I sat on the bed. I could make out the faint outline of her
body on the comforter. I touched it to see if her warmth was
still there, but the fabric had grown cold. I breathed in between
the pillows and picked up a hint of her scent. I grabbed the
book. On the page at which it had been left open, Tania had underlined a phrase with a blue marker—"Before being humans,
we're animals"—and on the margin, she had written in her uneven handwriting: "and even before that we're demons."

I LEFT THE ROOM and walked to the lobby. The motel was
empty. I was the only client, but still the neon "Motel Villalba"
sign kept blinking on the rooms. You could clearly hear the electric hum, like a nocturnal cicada.

The young man with curly hair nodded lazily on a sofa.
Upon hearing me walk in, he opened his eyes, gazed at me in a
stupor and suddenly shot up.

"Sorry chief, I dozed off there for a second," he said.

I asked him for the phone. I wanted to know if Tania had
made it home. I called and her mother answered, alarmed. I supposed Tania was still out so I hung up. I asked the kid if there
was a nearby pizza place that delivered. He said there were several, but that they all closed at eleven. In a corner I spotted a
crate of Cokes. I asked him to sell me one.

"No," he answered, "not to you. You're a client."

He opened one and picked up the bottle cap from the floor.

"Sometimes they've got prizes," he explained as he looked at it.

He gave me the soda and refused to accept a tip.

• • •

I WENT TO the car to pick up Gregorio's box. I could look through it until Tania got back, if she did. I put the Coke bottle on the roof of the car and looked for the keys in my pocket. While I did, I looked at the box lit by the neon blue and I clearly saw it move a few centimeters. I backed away from the car. I swallowed saliva. Uneasy, I drew close and looked through the window. The box was in its place and I laughed like an idiot, leaning on the hood.

I decided against looking through the box and, still a little frightened, I went back into the room. On the way I bumped into the dark-skinned guy who was wandering around the parking lot. I asked him to show me his revolver. He took it off his belt and removed the six bullets before he gave it to me.

"Sorry man," he said, pretending to be careful, "but you never know."

He gave me the gun. It was nice; a .22 Smith & Wesson, clean and well-kept. I offered to buy it from him.

"I can't do that; the boss'll kill me."

"I'll give you a thousand; what d'you say? I promise I'll get the money by tomorrow."

The offer sounded tempting.

"And what do I tell the boss?"

"Tell him someone stole it from you on the bus."

"No, he asks for it every day when he gets here and he keeps it locked up."

"Well, think about it."

"Sure thing."

He withdrew to continue his rounds and to think about how to swindle the gun from his boss.

• • •

I GOT TO THE ROOM and took off my jacket. I drank the soda and left the empty bottle on the carpet. I looked at myself in the mirror. A thin vein pulsed on my right temple. The bags under my eyes deepened near my eyelids. My hair was ruffled and messy. My face covered in stubble. And the blue shadow of the buffalo inside me, threatening me again.

I lay on the bed. On that same bed—the evening of the twenty-second of February—Tania and I made love for the first time. We did it clumsily, bewildered by the guilt and lack of experience. She was a virgin and, with the exception of two brief one-night stands, you could say I was as well.

We got tangled as we undressed. Her hair got hooked on my belt buckle, her blouse tore and two buttons popped off my shirt. We wanted to go fast and slow at the same time. We didn't know how to position ourselves and we just climbed on top of each other like mating turtles.

We tried several positions. In all of them Tania complained. "You're hurting me," she kept saying. After several attempts I managed to penetrate her. She moaned softly and looked at me differently than she usually did.

"You're inside," she murmured, "deep inside," and kissed me on the mouth. When we finished we held each other for a long time without moving. I felt her moist skin under the blankets, her breasts squeezing against my chest, her hair brushing against my face. I was surprised to be with her like this, in her complete nakedness. I had never been next to a fully naked woman. My two previous sexual encounters had been with half-dressed drunken girls, muddled fucks that hadn't lasted more than three minutes. The first was in the back of a pickup truck, in clear view of my friends, who huddled around and spied from a window; the second was in the hallway of an abandoned house, next door to my cousin Pilar's graduation party.

Tania and I caressed each other till we fell asleep. In the midst of the nap's stupor, I'd turn to look at her and then went back to sleep holding on to her naked torso.

We woke up after an hour.

"You snore," I said.

She just clicked her tongue.

"Quietly," I added, "you snore quietly . . . you lulled me to sleep."

With her eyes half-closed she smiled and kissed my forehead. Still slothful she sat up on the edge of the bed. She grabbed her bag and rummaged through it until she found a roll of LifeSavers. She unwrapped two of them, one green, one red, she held them in her hands and closed her fists.

"Which one?" she asked.

I chose the right hand and she showed me the red one.

"You get cherry." She put it on my tongue, and as she did I licked the tip of her fingers. She put the green one in her mouth and sucked on it, and then kissed me.

We exchanged candy and saliva. She pulled away, savored the candy again and raised her face, as if she were tasting wine.

"I was wrong," she said, smiling. "I think you got lime."

She turned her back to me. She closed her bag and put it on the nightstand. The thin hair on her shoulders shone golden in the evening light. I reached out and stroked the nape of her neck. She turned her head and caught my fingers.

"What are we going to do?" she asked.

I sat behind her and wrapped my arms around her waist. From a nearby radio I could hear some trendy pop song.

"I don't know," I answered.

"I wish this evening would never end," she whispered melancholically.

The next day we'd go back to the usual: she, to being Gregorio's girlfriend; me to being his best friend.

Tania stood up and walked confidently naked through the room. She stopped and crossed her arms, standing like someone waiting for a taxi.

"Aren't you coming?" she asked.

"Where?"

"To shower with me," she answered with certainty.

Her words disconcerted me. She had said them as if there had been an agreement between us, or a habit we'd both grown accustomed to. She seemed to pick up on my confusion.

"That's how they do it in the movies, isn't it?" she said.

She held out her hand to help me up. She pulled and the covers slipped onto the floor. On the mattress cover were two faint lines of blood. Tania walked up to them and examined them, intrigued.

"I'd heard it was supposed to hurt a lot the first time, but it's not that bad," she said.

"What are you talking about?" I asked, feigning ignorance.

"Don't you know?"

Several times, Tania had insisted she was a virgin. I didn't really believe her: Gregorio was too obsessive not to have fucked her. But I honestly didn't care if she was or not.

"I told you I don't give a damn about that," I asserted.

"You don't, but I do."

She put her arms around my neck and led me backward into the bathroom.

• • •

WE MADE LOVE AGAIN in the shower, spread out over the tiles, the hot water on our backs, not worrying about using a condom, unafraid of pregnancy, unafraid of ourselves or of what would eventually happen.

I stroked her body inch by inch. I tried to impregnate myself with her, to have her on my fingertips, in case what happened that evening never happened again.

Night fell. We agreed that she'd leave the motel first. I wouldn't leave the bathroom until I heard her walk out. This, we thought, would diminish the guilt. We'd been secretly seeing each other for six months. We'd meet after school (Gregorio had already been kicked out of high school, which made things easier) and drive away in her car to distant areas south of the city—the kind that still have empty lots and half-built houses. There we'd kiss for half an hour, only to go back to our houses as soon as we were done.

These escapades became more and more frequent until we assumed it was inevitable that we should sleep together, which happened on the twenty-second of February.

Tania stepped out of the shower, wrapped herself in a towel, and walked out without saying a word. Glum, I stayed under the water, waiting for her to leave, imagining her naked in the room, calmly naked.

I opened the small window above the soap dish to let the steam out. The sky was clear with ecstatic, sparse clouds. On the radio, after a stupid, catchy song, the DJ announced the exact time in an affected voice: It was seven minutes past eight at night. One song later I heard Tania's car drive through the parking lot.

I shut off the shower and, still wet, walked into the room. I looked around—everything and nothing of her was left behind:

the towel with which she dried herself left on the dresser; her wet footsteps vanishing in the carpet; a hairbrush she left next to the mirror, and the disheveled bed where, a few hours earlier, we'd made love.

I sat on the mattress. On the sheet, next to the bloodstains, Tania had written in black marker: "I love you more than you think."

I tore the sheet with my teeth and took the piece of cloth with her blood on it.

AT THREE IN THE MORNING I decided to leave room 803. I was exhausted and wanted to go home and sleep. Nothing indicated that Tania would be back and she probably had gone back home already.

I put my jacket on and wrote down on a piece of paper: "Tania, if you come back, please stay here," and I put it next to the book. Thunder rumbled and the window shook. I looked out: lightning flashed inside the dark clouds.

I opened the door. The dark-skinned man patrolled the parking lot sheathed in a gray raincoat. In the distance he signaled me with his flashlight and walked over with small steps.

"How's it going? You leaving?"

"Yeah."

He raised his eyes and looked up at the sky.

"Well, with the storm that's coming, if I were you I'd stay in the room."

"I've gotta go, man."

He scratched his head with the hand holding the flashlight.

"What do I tell the girl if she comes back?"

"Don't tell her anything."

A car appeared at the entrance. The man showed them the way with the flashlight and guided them to room 810.

The motel had only thirteen rooms. The "8" before each number was a flourish by the owner.

I got into my car just when the rain broke loose. I turned on the headlights. In the beams, I could see the dark-skinned man charging a fat man the ninety-peso fee.

I DROVE IN THE MIDDLE of a storm that caused flooding and blackouts in several areas of the city. Even with the windshield wipers at full speed, visibility was nil. In some places, the waterline rose over the sidewalks and it was impossible to go any farther.

A few blocks away from home, an ambulance passed me with its turrets lit and pulled over next to an upturned VT Beetle. I lowered my speed, opened the window, and drove slowly past the accident. A few curious bystanders, enduring the cold and the rain, surrounded a body covered by a coat and a girl with a bloodied face who stared, absorbed, at the body splayed on the pavement. No one, not even the paramedics, paid attention to her.

I stopped and asked a man if there was anything I could do to help. He gave me a hostile look and shook his head. I insisted, but he wasn't paying attention anymore.

I swerved around the broken glass scattered on the asphalt and drove down a dark street, intermittently lit by the ambulance lights.

I FELT COMFORTED as soon as I drove the car into the garage. The rain, the street, and the night were locked outside. I took

Gregorio's box and headed to the kitchen. I ate two bananas, a bunch of grapes, a fistful of chocolates and drank a carton of milk.

I went up the stairs two steps at a time. My father was waiting for me in front of my room.

"Are you okay?" he asked.

I nodded. He patted me on the shoulder.

"Good night. Get some rest."

I watched him as he walked across the corridor. It couldn't be that this slightly hunched man with skinny legs and a spreading bald spot was a traitor, as Gregorio invariably claimed. He never was. He never betrayed me, not even in the most difficult moments of all that.

He stopped in the middle of the hall and turned to look at me.

"It's late. Go to bed," he ordered with the same indulgent tone with which he used to send me to bed when I was a boy.

"I'm going," I answered.

He raised his hand to say good night and headed back to his room. And no, he wasn't a traitor.

I PUT THE BOX on a chair, but as I untied my sneakers it kept attracting my attention, so I decided to hide it in the closet.

I got undressed and put on flannel pajamas. They were worn and patched and used to belong to my father. I rescued them when he tried to throw them away. I didn't want them to end up in the garbage, or as cloth for cleaning windows. They were too linked to him.

I got in between the sheets. I'd recently changed them and they were still stiff from the starch. I liked them that way. On several occasions I'd asked my mother not to put any softener in after washing them. The same went for my towels, shirts, and

42

underwear. I liked to feel the fibers lightly scratch my skin, especially when I slid my feet into bed. It relaxed me.

That night, however, I slept restlessly. I constantly woke up with the feeling that a large and angry animal was breathing beside me. I'd hear it snort, its hot exhalation, and I'd sit up and open my eyes. The huffing would extinguish itself in the dark. There was nothing in the room. The animal was breathing inside me. I knew that it was just a bad dream polluted by Gregorio's dementia, a cheap hallucination, or at least that's what I wanted to believe.

Some years earlier, Gregorio had called me at five in the morning from the mental hospital. It was back when he wasn't yet kept in the restricted areas. He spoke to me in a low voice and urgently asked me to go see him.

I eluded the night watchmen and arrived at his room. I found him next to his bed, watching the dawn through the window. I greeted him without caution. Gregorio didn't answer the greeting and without turning to look at me, started to talk, emphasizing every word.

"The night buffalo dreams of us," he said.

The buffalos and cryptic tone seemed to be his latest obsessions. I joked about it:

"They're called bison, not buffalo."

I laughed. His attitude was too serious, too affected, especially dressed in his ridiculous little blue robe.

"Are you making fun of me?" he asked, looking at me askance.

"No," I answered and laughed again.

He spun around and with one abrupt movement grabbed me by my shirt collar. He pulled his face up to mine and I stopped laughing. For the first time, his gaze intimidated me.

"The night buffalo is going to dream of you," he said. "He'll run next to you, you'll hear his hooves and his breath. You'll smell his sweat and he'll come so close you'll almost be able to touch him. And when the buffalo decides to attack, you'll wake up on the fields of death. Then you'll stop making fun, you son of a bitch."

His threat seemed real.

"So¿" I asked wryly.

He pulled me even closer.

"The night buffalo is inside me now. He's been dreaming of me for fifty, a hundred weeks, and I don't know how to get him out, Manuel, I don't know how."

"They're nightmares."

"No," he answered ardently, "the buffalo is the beginning of my end."

He loosened his grip but didn't let go of me. We were silent for a few moments, looking straight at each other's eyes. A nurse walked in with some medication and, upon seeing me, exclaimed, annoyed, that visiting hours didn't start until nine.

"Is that all you have to say to me¿" I asked Gregorio.

He let go of my shirt and moistened his lips.

"Yeah, that's it."

The nurse started to lecture.

"Young man, I've told you . . ."

I walked past the woman, paying her no attention, and she shut up. I headed toward the door. Before crossing the threshold, Gregorio called out to me:

"Manuel . . ."

I turned to look at him.

"Don't say I didn't warn you."

• • •

ALTHOUGH I WAS AFRAID of Gregorio's threat for a few months, as time went on I began to think of the night buffalo as one of his several delusions. I didn't dream of the buffalo, and, in that case, it didn't dream of me.

But in that early-morning restlessness I was overcome with the certainty that a massive animal was breathing inside me. If that wasn't the case, what the hell was that angry snorting?

I turned on the lights in my room and checked the grates and windows to rule out a draft. Anxious, I paced back and forth. I tried to calm down. The same thing happened when I dreamt of earwigs. I felt them running through my veins, gnawing through my flesh, and when I woke up they were gone. There was nothing. Nothing. Why worry about a panting animal? No, there was no buffalo. Nor would there be. There wouldn't be any more Gregorio either. He was dead, charred, reduced to blue smoke and ashes, rotting God knows where. It had all been a crass nightmare.

AT EIGHT IN THE MORNING, my brother Luis came into my room. He shook me several times.

"Wake up, wake up . . ."

I registered his voice as something distant and uncertain.

"What's the matter?" I managed to mouth heavily.

"You've got a phone call."

"Who?"

He put the mouthpiece next to my pillow and walked out. It was Tania's mother. Sobbing, she explained that her daughter still hadn't come home and she suspected another prolonged disappearance. I promised I'd help her look.

I tried to sleep a little more but couldn't. Tania's absence wouldn't let me. I loved her—I loved her very much—but it was hard to decipher her. I decided to go back to room 803. I couldn't think of anywhere else to look.

I showered with my eyes closed, leaning against the wall, dazed by sleep deprivation. Without the energy to pick out new clothes, I put on the ones from the day before. I grabbed whatever money I could get my hands on. I had no car that morning and I planned to take a taxi. I was in no condition to travel around the city in public transport.

I arrived at the motel just before nine-thirty. The sky had cleared a little and a weak sun could be traced through the clouds. Mr. Camariña was already working in his office. Upon seeing me walk by he nodded hello. I responded similarly. In one of the driveways, Pancho was mopping the tiles on the floor. He recognized me from afar and walked over.

"Hey, Manuel."

"Hey."

"D'you want me to open or do you have your keys?"

"You open."

After that twenty-second of February, Tania and I started to go to the motel more and more frequently—three, four, even five times a week—always in Tania's car, always her paying, because she could. If when we got to the motel, room 803 was occupied, we would leave; we had made love in 803 for the first time and we didn't plan on doing it in any other room.

One afternoon Mr. Camariña intercepted us. He said he'd seen us there on several occasions and he mentioned our predilection for room 803. We were disconcerted; we thought of ourselves as fleeting clients, almost invisible. Camariña proposed a deal: Instead of the ninety pesos a day, he offered us

803, exclusively, as many times as we wanted to use it, for a two-thousand-peso monthly rent. It was Tania's decision; there was no way I could afford that kind of money. She accepted. From then on we took over the room and made it our own, not only to make love in, but also to study in, rest in, or just to get away from everyone else.

PANCHO UNLOCKED the door and pushed it open.

"Tania hasn't been here?" I asked.

"No, I haven't seen her, at least since I got here."

The dark-skinned man and the kid with curly hair were nowhere to be seen.

"Did the guys from the other shift leave yet?"

"The new guys? Since seven."

"They didn't leave you any messages for me?"

"No."

The room was in exactly the same mess I'd left it in. They hadn't made the beds or cleaned the bathroom yet. A single file of ants marched down the side of the wall and gathered around the Cock-Cola bottle I'd left on the carpet. The ants were tiny and they blackened the mouth of the bottle. When I was a boy I used to play God with them. I'd randomly kill some. That way I'd let a few, the minority, crawl away without my finger squashing them. This was my version of divinity.

I took the bottle, set it outside the room next to some potted plants and let them all live.

I LAY ON THE BED. Where could Tania be? I couldn't tell and, at this point, to consider the zoo or airport as possibilities was absurd. I had no choice but to wait for her to reappear in her usual surreptitious, unexpected way.

I took my clothes off—to do that in 803 was a way of being with her—put my hands behind my head and fell asleep. Real sleep; no panting animals, no earwigs, no phone calls.

I woke up not knowing what time it was. I assumed it was late since the sunlight was filtering through the blinds on my right. I must have been cold while I was asleep, because I woke up wrapped in the comforter.

Some woman, probably a waitress, walked down the hallway humming a song I didn't recognize. It was an old, sweet tune, strange to the sordid block of motel rooms.

I put on my T-shirt and pants and walked barefoot to the edge of the parking lot. The wind was blowing and in the sky the clouds were gathering rapidly. I spotted Pancho at the entrance to 807. He was tying up a bundle of sheets and dirty towels. I whistled to him.

"Do you want your room cleaned now?" he asked as he approached.

"No, I want you to do me a favor."

"Name it."

"Could you go to the front desk and order me a large ham pizza and three sodas?"

"Don Polo's sandwiches are much better, just round the corner," he suggested.

"No," I answered, "I've been craving pizza since last night."

He shook his head in disapproval. I gave him a hundred-peso bill and went back inside. I didn't plan on leaving for the rest of the evening. I wasn't going to look for Tania, I wasn't going to try to call her, and I wasn't going to worry about her, at least for the next two hours.

I took my clothes off again and started to thumb through the Ruvalcaba book. Tania had underlined a few phrases with a red pen, seemingly at random. There was no connection between them. I was particularly interested in the fact that on page eighty-six she underlined: "The bureaucrats, upon leaving their offices, would stop to buy bread to take home." And on the top of the page she wrote, with exclamation marks: "look!" "look!" "look!"

What the hell did these phrases mean to her? What did she have to do with bureaucrats and their grayness? I got the feeling the passage held the key to her disappearances. And the jealousy came back, the clumsy jealousy from years before.

Jealousy: I would go to the motel so often, alone or with Tania, that I became a familiar face to the employees. Pancho was the youngest of them—he was my age. He came to work early and left at dusk. He did everything: cleaned the rooms, charged the clients, washed the linen, counted the towels (he had to go into the rooms as soon as the clients left to make sure they hadn't stolen any), and worked in the reception. He was attentive and hardworking, and I liked him the best.

At first we'd greet each other with tepid, formal gestures. He'd glance at me out of the corner of his eye, following motel rules. His attitude changed a little when I introduced myself to him and asked him his name. Even though the relationship became friendlier, he was still prudent—you never know what to expect with motel clients.

As time went by we started a small friendship. We'd occasionally chat in the five- or ten-minute breaks he had every four hours.

One evening when I showed up alone, I noticed Pancho was more reserved than usual. He avoided me and was terse. He acted like this for several days. He'd answer my questions about his behavior with a curt "Nothing's wrong." Until, one evening, he decided to reveal why.

"Manuel, can I tell you something? But you have to promise you won't get pissed off," he asked, unsure of himself.

"Sure, man."

"But really, promise, because if anything happens I'll get fired for opening my mouth."

"I swear."

Pancho breathed in deeply.

"It's just that . . ." he said and stopped short.

He breathed in again.

"No, I shouldn't."

"Come on, man, this is getting boring."

He shook his head. I gestured for him to go on.

He looked me in the eyes, gulped, and suddenly let it out:

"Okay, here goes: Your girl came by twice last week with the guy she used to come here with."

"Used to? When?"

"Before she came with you."

I was stunned, dumfounded. Pancho went on: They had come to the motel eight or ten times and always stayed in room 803. The description of Tania's companion fit Gregorio feature by feature.

The disclosure overwhelmed me. All of a sudden my relationship with Tania took on a fraudulent aspect. What was Tania's double game about? What was she plotting? Why had she insisted on feeding me the stupid myth of her virginity?

I left the motel furious. "So that's why the bitch paid for the room," I brayed, "that's why, goddammit."

• • •

I WALKED AROUND THE CITY for hours on a chaotic, furious excursion. What game was that slut playing?

I confronted her the next day, shouting, minutes before class. At first she just listened. Then she timidly tried to defend herself, but every time she tried to explain her motives I'd shut her up with insults.

Tania ended up irate and ended the argument when, abrupt and arrogant, she said that for all intents and purposes Gregorio was her boyfriend, that she was not committed to me and that she could do whatever she goddamn well pleased. We broke up (our romance? our affair? our sexual merry-go-round?) amid shoves and curses.

I sank into a state of paranoid jealousy, weathering our love's decay, the insecurity, the doubt. Now, three years later, was it worth getting jealous over half a paragraph that spoke of bureaucrats buying bread? No, it wasn't worth it, especially after all the effort it took to piece the relationship back together.

I PUT RUVALCABA'S book down and fell asleep. A while later, what seemed a short while, someone knocked on the door. Groggy, I wrapped myself in a towel and looked through the peephole. Pancho was balancing the items in his hands, trying to keep them from falling. I opened and he handed over the food, together with the bill and change. Since he refused to accept a tip I gave him one of the sodas and a slice of pizza.

I devoured the pizza and could have eaten three more. Parched, I drank down both sodas, one after the other, and then drank tap water till I was ready to burst.

I had dreams in the short nap Pancho interrupted. I was unable to remember any of them, but I was left with a residue of sadness. Besides Gregorio and Tania's absence, I was heavy with something like an absence of myself. I had turned into someone different from whom I thought I would become.

Naked, I walked to the window that looked out onto the parking lot. I discreetly pushed the curtain aside. The evening had turned brown. Gusts of wind blew pieces of paper over the houses and the rain threatened to come down any minute.

A black luxury car crossed the parking lot and stopped in the driveway to room 810. That made eleven occupied rooms. Almost full. This happened Friday afternoons, especially fortnightly, on payday. Couples would come in and hole up for the weekend. There were students, workers, bodyguards, maids, stuck-up ladies, bank clerks, bureaucrats (would they have gone to the motel before, or after buying bread for their homes?), nervous teenagers, taxi drivers, cops. Despite its diverse clientele, the Motel Villalba took pride in being a moral motel: Access was denied to prostitutes, gay couples, anyone under fifteen, and threesomes. "One guy and two dresses make messes" was one of Mr. Camariña's mottos.

Even though it was a cheap, shoddy motel, the rooms were clean and the furniture in good condition. The mattresses were old, but still firm; the headboards were fastened solidly and didn't creak with the typical rocking; the dresser benches and chairs didn't wobble and the mirrors weren't peeling; the carpets were constantly washed and vacuumed; the sheets were immediately changed after use and there was no need to fear lying down on viscous stains; the comforters had no cigarette burns. It was a different motel from the ones I'd been to with Margarita or other women. "All love, no matter how dirty," claimed Mr. Camariña, "deserves a clean place."

Nor was it a motel with a dark past or bad reputation. Other than an incident in which a woman in her fifties sliced her lover's legs with a knife (a young waiter who was cheating on her with someone else), there had been no bloody acts of violence. No murder, suicide, or gunfight.

Gregorio took Tania to the Motel Villalba for the first time by mistake. He thought it was one where an army lieutenant and his lover (the wife of one of his friends) had committed suicide together. It had been a story widely covered on the front pages of the tabloids Gregorio liked so much.

He had read that the motel was in the Portales neighborhood, and that the room number ended in 3. He searched for it in order to consummate his love with Tania in the same place where the lieutenant and his lover had sealed theirs in blood. He was way off: The Villalba motel was twenty blocks away.

So, there were no suicide rooms for Gregorio. Neither was there consummation. He had Tania as naked as I did. He caressed her, kissed her, drank her. He lay on the same bed as I did. He slept with her, bathed with her, but was unable to enter her. Not the first, not the second, not the fifth time around. He, the first of us who fucked, he who had penetrated so many, couldn't, back then, make love to the woman he loved the most.

And I imagine them both: he, in a corner of the room, naked, sweaty, defeated, with her beside him, also naked, trying to console him, kissing his forehead, with him collapsed and certain that thousands of earwigs are devouring him day after day, hour after hour, and that these same earwigs are piling up at the tip of his penis ready to emerge with his semen into her, to invade and devour her, as they do him, and she trying to convince him that it won't happen. And I imagine them both, crying, naked, in a corner of room 803.

• • •

I LEFT THE MOTEL exactly at nightfall, at "zero hour." "It's the most dangerous hour to drive on the highway," my father used to say when we traveled by car. "It's the hour when you can still see, but you don't know what you're looking at."

I counted my leftover change. It wasn't enough for a taxi. I walked to the corner, where a group of poor women, workers, builders, and night-school students waited for the bus. It was a compact, silent group, whose faces were now barely discernible.

It started to drizzle and we all stuck to the wall trying to avoid getting wet. Pointless. A sudden downpour started and the wind carried it into us.

Most of them ran to take refuge in a nearby taco joint on the other side of the street. I stayed on the corner, next to a short, bony old woman who, clothed only in a worn blue sweater, weathered the rain, awaiting the bus.

No matter how much I tried to stop it with my hands, the rain filtered down my neck, into my back. Why was it raining so much in February? The meteorologists on television attributed it to global warming. This did not seem to concern the old woman beside me, who stared imperturbably in the direction from which the bus would be coming.

A blue car pulled over next to us. The driver honked the horn. I squinted through the windows, but couldn't tell who it was. I stopped paying attention to him. The driver insisted. I walked over and recognized Camariña's completely bald head as he gestured for me to get in.

I jumped into the car. As soon as I sat down, the car seat got wet. Embarrassed, I apologized.

"Don't worry about it," answered Camariña, "it'll dry off later."

He pulled away. Through the window I watched the old

woman who, dripping wet, remained impassively waiting for her bus.

"Where are you going?" asked Camariña.

"Villa Verdún."

"Where's that?"

"Far away, all the way up Calzada de las Águilas. Which way are you headed?"

"I'm taking you home," he said.

I tried to protest. Camariña stopped me: "You're one of my two best clients, kid. What're you gonna do?"

HE DROVE SILENTLY for a while. The slow, anarchic traffic didn't seem to bother him. Every now and then he'd drum his fingers on the steering wheel to the rhythm of a song on the radio. His forearms were thick and strong. His hands were meaty, with thick, jutting veins. His stubby fingers seemed more like a mechanic's than a motel owner's.

Camariña skipped the line of cars by turning the wrong way into a one-way avenue, and then zigzagged through narrow, nameless streets. He cut through several blocks and joined the traffic farther ahead. He looked at me with childish pride.

"At this point I know this city better than my hometown."

His hometown was Villalba, in Galicia, near the sea. He'd come to Mexico thirty-five years ago, when he was eighteen. He set up the motel under the premise that there are four basic human needs: "housing, clothing, feeding, and fucking." Camariña laughed his horselike laugh every time he mentioned this. On several occasions he had invited me into his office for a chat. Despite his wryness he truly enjoyed conversation.

Upon reaching Insurgentes Avenue I realized that a bus was

driving past us heading to my house. I tried to get ready to board it.

"No, kid, I'll take you."

"You've got me close enough. I don't want to make you go out of your way."

Camariña leaned over and shut the door I'd half opened.

We went on. Camariña turned off the radio and started to talk about football, his greatest passion. In Mexico he was a Necaxa fan, in Spain a Sporting fan. He knew statistics for each team and player, tactical formations, the starting lineups for every first division team. He told lively stories of games he never saw. His football world was completely separate from the world of furtive love affairs that unfolded in the rooms of his motel.

We stopped at a light and, out of the blue, he asked if I'd had a fight with Tania. I said no.

"It's just that in the evening your girlfriend drove into the business." Camariña always called it the business, never the motel. "She stopped in front of the room, stood there for a while, then turned around and left. And since you've been in there alone, I just thought . . ."

I felt a sudden uneasiness, a ventral oppression. Tania was avoiding me. She was avoiding me again.

Camariña noticed the state I was in and squeezed my leg with his great hand.

"Don't worry, women are like that. That's why the only woman I've ever dealt with is my wife and she's more than enough."

TANIA GAVE THE IMPRESSION of being a woman permanently trying to escape. Running seemed the only constant thing about her. Many confused this trait for betrayal, even me. But that wasn't true. Tania had a profound sense of loyalty. That was what had made her go back to 803 with Gregorio. She tried to counteract the guilt by giving Gregorio her body or, specifically, the opportunity her body meant. Not her love, because she loved me. But she cared for Gregorio and the way he was collapsing into madness kept her in constant pain.

Reconciliation with Tania was tough and hard-fought. Despite the fact that during the four months we were apart we loved each other more than ever, we never stopped humiliating and hurting each other. We got back together without having gotten over our grudges. We were always holding petty things against each other and we fought cruelly only to stop seeing each other for days. Then she'd avoid me and her absence caused a pressure in my stomach.

We brought things back to normal after getting tired of hurting each other. She remained Gregorio's girlfriend for almost another year and a half, loving him dearly and assiduously. She used to visit him in the hospital after leaving the motel, still impregnated with the sweat of our orgasms.

I thought we were fooling Gregorio. Never. From the very beginning he had intuited our affair, and he dedicated himself to harassing us with subtle, understated, devastating blows. He ambushed our relationship at will, awakening guilt, kindling jealousy, stirring up conflict. He'd hit us when we least expected it. Tania and I resisted, I don't know if it was because we were naive, or because we really loved each other that much.

CAMARIÑA LOOKED WORRIED about how I reacted to his question about Tania and spent the rest of the ride trying to comfort me.

He complimented the jacket Margarita's father had lent me.

"You don't know how long I've been looking for one like that," he said as he felt the waterproof fabric with his mechanic's fingers, "it must be really warm."

Then he started joking around. He managed to make me laugh with the list of objects left behind in the motel rooms: icons of the Virgin of Guadalupe, gold chains, key chains, portfolios, books, baby bottles, purses, vibrators, and even a laptop computer. That's without counting the unopened condoms, tubes of vaginal lubricant, aromatic essences, tattered underwear, and brushes.

He told me that the clients rarely returned for their possessions, especially if they were valuable and belonged to middle-class or "nice" people. They could tolerate going to a motel where their relationship was covered up by employees who didn't look them in the eye and the discretion of the driveway curtains. But it was a very different thing to come face-to-face with a man who, garrisoned behind a counter, would ask them what he could do for them. It was a risk they simply would not take.

"These clients," Camariña told me, "need something like a wrestling mask."

After an hour, Camariña dropped me at home. Before we got out he patted me on the shoulder just like my father used to do.

"Cheer up, kid. You may not get enough of one woman, but love never runs out, understand?"

"No."

"What I'm trying to say is that there are plenty of women."

I smiled and got out of the car. Camariña turned, drove past me, and waved good-bye. I ran up to him and knocked on the window. He stopped abruptly.

"What's up?" he asked, puzzled.

I pointed at my jacket.

"You like it?"

"Yeah, it's very nice."

I took it off and pushed it through the window.

"What are you doing?" he asked.

"I'm giving it to you."

Camariña blushed a Spanish red.

"I won't allow it," he said and almost threw it out of the car.

"I won't either," I answered. I bundled up the jacket and threw into the far end of the backseat.

"I didn't bring you to your house for you to give me presents," he argued, "I'm not your darling."

I leaned on the edge of the door.

"You may not have enough cold," I said, "but you can never have too many jackets."

"What d'you mean?"

"That I've got lots of jackets."

Camariña smiled and smacked me upside the head.

"Thanks," he said wryly and drove down the street.

I'd find a way to get another jacket or I'd make up an excuse for Margarita's dad.

NOBODY WAS HOME. My parents had gone to dinner with some friends and Luis was in Cuernavaca for the weekend. My mother had left me a plate of chicken sandwiches in the kitchen for dinner. I settled into a chair by the kitchen table and grabbed my message book—and I say "my" because at home everyone had their own. In these was a meticulous register of every phone call: who'd called, at what time, and why. Everyone had to jot these details down in the corresponding message book. It was a mania my mother had acquired when she was the personal assistant to the minister of finance.

Tania's mother had called eight times: three in the morning, two at midday, two in the afternoon, and the last one at seven thirty-six. All eight calls had the same message: "Do you know anything about Tania?" I looked at the clock: quarter to nine. According to the intervals at which she'd called, she'd call again at about ten-thirty.

There was also a call from Rebecca at five-fifteen. She was a classmate from college with whom I occasionally had sex; she was wondering why I hadn't been to class. A call from Margarita at five past six, asking me to call her. And another, which surprised me, from Dr. Macías, the doctor who had carried out, with evident success, what he called "the process of Gregorio's therapeutic rehabilitation" (how many suicides must it have taken to bolster his prestige as a psychiatrist?). He'd called twice, and left the numbers for his office and beeper. He'd probably called to offer his services.

I TOOK A BITE of one of the sandwiches, but pushed it aside: It had a layer of onions. My mother still confused which of her sons liked onions and which one did not.

I made myself some cereal and sat down to watch television. I turned to one of the cable channels and watched, uninterested. I switched it off and went into my room to try to read a novel. I couldn't concentrate.

I dialed Rebecca's number. She had a dull boyfriend and was in love with me. She was pretty and I was attracted to her. She answered and upon hearing my voice said, "You've got the wrong number, miss," and hung up. She would always do that when her dull boyfriend was there. This weighed on me—it would've been a good night to go to the movies and make love to her in her car.

Margarita's phone was busy the five times I tried to call her. Then I spoke to Tania's mother. She answered on the first ring. She sounded worried. She wasn't a bad person. Perhaps a little frivolous, but kind and attentive. Tania's father was a labor lawyer with a reputation for winning cases by corrupting union leaders and sabotaging strikes with scabs. But he was nice to me.

Both were certain that Tania would come back. They had no doubts, but the wait was wearing them away. "One more of these days, Manuel, and I'm going to die," she said between sobs. I was tempted to tell her: One more of these days and I'll kill your daughter. I didn't plan on saying this as a joke. No, because I truly believed it. To kill her so her disappearances wouldn't kill me so much anymore.

I COULDN'T BEAR BEING home alone. Since the rain had stopped, I decided to go out. I walked around and around until I got bored. I had no money to go to a movie or to a cafeteria for a drink. I walked over to the basketball courts in the middle of the park. I'd won some money there betting on one-on-ones. Not much: twenty, thirty pesos a game. Enough. If it weren't a rainy evening I'd have found someone to play. Instead, I found a bunch of teenagers getting drunk on beer. They'd driven a car up next to the bleachers and opened all four doors so the tape deck could be heard full blast. The drunkest of them flailed around to the beat of some monotonous rap music.

They weren't gang members; they were middle-class mama's boys whose idea of a wild party was smashing bottles against the floor and vomiting behind the baskets. I recognized three or four of them and walked over. Maybe they could lend me some money.

"What's up, Michael Jordan?" was the greeting I got from the one they called Tommy. I'd won some money off of him a few times at basketball.

"What's going on?" I answered.

Tommy offered me a beer.

"I don't drink," I said.

"You ain't got any vices?" one of them asked.

"Yeah, different vices," I answered, "better ones."

The one they called Pony opened his hand and showed me a joint.

"Are you into this vice, or is it too rough for you?" he asked sarcastically. He felt he was the leader of the gang.

"No, I don't do that either. I don't have teenage vices," I answered.

The others mocked him, celebrating my joke. I looked for a dry spot in the bleachers and sat next to Tommy.

"What's up with you guys?" I asked them.

"Just hanging out, drinking," answered Beaver, the shortest of them all.

The tape finished and the drunk who'd been dancing alone shouted for them to put the rap back on. Since nobody paid attention to him, he stumbled over to the car, threw himself onto the front seat and fiddled with the knobs on the stereo. The rap started playing again and the drunk jumped out of the car to spin on his axis and stare at the moon.

"What about you? What're you doing over here?" asked Tommy.

"I came to see if I could find someone to play some ball with."

Beaver pointed at the soaked courts.

"You must mean water polo . . ."

Several of them feigned laughter, Pony more than the others.

"Where's the guy you used to come with?" asked a blond kid they called Pretty Boy.

"Who?"

"The tall guy with a tattoo like yours," he explained.

"He's dead," I said.

Everyone laughed again, as if I'd said something really funny. I laughed, too.

"Really," I said, still laughing, and put my index finger on my eyebrow, "he cracked a bullet right through here last Tuesday."

Some laughed, some didn't. They didn't know if I was being funny or serious.

"Are you fucking with us?" asked Tommy.

"Not at all."

They all looked at me, shocked, except for the one dancing drunk with the moon.

"How d'you like my friend's vices?" I added and looked at Pony.

There was no one to celebrate the joke. I half smiled. The others remained silent. The tape ended and the drunk started shouting again. He was silenced by a fat guy, big and ugly, who I hadn't realized was there.

"Quit it, Yo-yo," he said, "I'm fucking sick of you."

He went to the car, took the key out of the ignition, and put it away.

"The music's over," he decided.

The drunk stared at him, glassy-eyed, with his arms open like a scarecrow. He complained under his breath and went to go collapse at the far end of the bleachers.

LITTLE BY LITTLE the group started to disperse. Pony walked away with his hands in his jacket pockets and started chatting with Beaver.

The fat guy and Pretty Boy sat down next to Tommy and me. They opened a few beers and drank them in slow gulps. They started talking about cars, cylinders and other idiocies. The fat guy, full of himself, walked over to his car and opened the hood to show us the motor. He proudly showed us hoses, spark plugs, hubcaps. I seized the moment to ask Tommy to lend me fifty pesos. He rummaged through his pockets and pulled out a ten-peso coin.

"It's all I've got," he explained.

I also asked Pretty Boy. He opened his wallet and, with his back to me, pulled out a twenty.

"I can lend you some more tomorrow," he said.

"I need them now," I told him, "for the cab and the movie ticket."

"You want to go to the movies?" asked the fat guy.

I nodded.

"What about you?" I asked the other two.

They also nodded. The fat man walked over to the car, poked around inside the glove compartment, and stood up with a look of satisfaction and two hundred-peso bills in his hand.

"I'm buyin'."

The four of us got into the car. I was in the copilot's seat. The fat guy floored the accelerator and we drove through the courts as the others jumped to one side.

He tried to take a shortcut through the park, where the terrain was muddier. The car skidded toward the trees without us hitting any of them. We left the park and exited onto an adjacent street that took us to Las Águilas Avenue.

The fat guy drove with just one hand. He ignored traffic lights, didn't stop for speed bumps, and passed other cars on their right at high speed. The two guys in the back seemed used to the driving and weren't the least bit fazed.

In the distance I noticed a patrol car with its turret off. I persuaded the fat guy to let me drive. They could stop us and his breath stank of beer. He pulled over and I sighed in relief when he let me take the wheel.

WE ARRIVED AT ONE of those buildings that hold ten movie theaters, record stores, and restaurants. There was a large selection of movies at eleven-thirty. I suggested we see *Mariposa Negra,* directed by Busi Cortés, which had just come out. The others were bent on watching a cheap action flick. Since I didn't have any money, I had to go along with their decision.

We got the tickets twenty minutes before the show. To kill time we went to read magazines at Sanborn's. The fat guy and Tommy soon got bored and decided to go to a liquor store to buy three small flasks of rum.

"You can drink real chill inside the theater," said the fat guy.

I was left alone with Pretty Boy. He was blond, handsome, and looked like a nice guy. He was as harmless as the rest of his friends. I asked him for the twenty pesos he was going to lend me earlier so I could buy a hunting magazine. He turned to his left and, taking cover, discreetly opened his wallet. Even so, I could tell it had more than a hundred pesos in it.

Pretty Boy held out a twenty-peso bill, and when he was about to put the wallet away I asked him for another twenty.

"It's all I've got," he said in a tone of voice that indicated otherwise.

"Don't bullshit me, I just saw you're carrying more."

He looked at me mortified, as if I were a teacher who'd caught him cheating on a test.

"It's the money my mom gave me to buy books for school," he said, hesitant.

"Don't worry," I said, "I'll pay you back by Sunday at the latest."

With a mousy motion he half-opened his wallet again and gave me another twenty.

"Thanks," I said, and put the bill in my pocket.

He was greedy and a liar; I wouldn't pay him back.

THE FAT GUY INSISTED we sit in the front of the theater. I refused but we ended up settling near the front row anyway.

The three of them started to drink from their flasks before the lights dimmed. The fat guy had even snuck in a liter of tequila bundled in his clothes. They were planning on drinking as if they were at a football match.

I was sick and tired of the movie after twenty minutes. I wasn't in the mood for gunshots, flying kicks, karate, and drunken teenagers. I whispered to Tommy that I was going to the bathroom and that I'd be right back. I left the theater and went back into Sanborn's.

I asked for a chocolate milk shake at the soda fountain. Some guy came over to my table and stared at me for a few seconds.

"Manuel?" he asked.

It was Ricardo Galindo, an old classmate of Gregorio's and mine in secondary and high school.

"Don't you recognize me?" he asked.

Of course I recognized him. He spent his time bullying Gregorio during the three years of secondary school, when Gregorio was skinny and shy.

"Sure, you're Ricardo," I answered.

He smiled and then put on a serious expression.

"I heard about Gregorio, I was really shocked."

"What happened?" I asked.

"Don't you know?"

I shook my head. Ricardo put his hand on the chair back and leaned in toward me.

"He committed suicide," he whispered.

I feigned surprise.

"Isn't that awful," he said with a pained face.

It couldn't have bothered him that much. One morning, as usual, Ricardo was making fun of Gregorio in the middle of bio lab. Gregorio, who by then had begun to change, smiled and took the scalpel we were using to dissect a rabbit. He stood next to Ricardo, held the blade to his throat, and forced him to walk backward through the rows of desks. And to the amazement of the professor and the other students, he leaned him against a wall and made an incision on his jaw. A small line of blood jumped and Gregorio lowered the scalpel. "One more time, you bastard, just one more time," he warned, "and I'll have your eyes." He turned around and sat down again. The next day he was suspended for a week.

"When did he kill himself?" I asked.

He shrugged his shoulders. Some girl gestured impatiently at him from a distance and he signaled "just a minute."

"Are you still Tania's boyfriend?"

I nodded. He remained silent, not knowing what else to say.

"Did you go to the movies?" he asked after a few seconds.

"Yes," I answered.

"What did you see?"

"*Mariposa Negra.*"

"How is it?"

"Really good. I highly recommend it."

He said good-bye exaggerating the pleasure it had given him to see me and skipped away between the tables toward the young woman waiting for him.

I TOOK THE ELEVATOR down to the parking lot. Once in the fat guy's car I realized that I didn't have any extra money with which to pay for the parking. Luckily they gave me two free hours for being a Sanborn's customer.

The city was almost empty. Strange, for a Friday. Maybe the rain had driven the night owls away.

The fat guy's car was fast. It was a red sports car, with aerodynamic contours, of some unimportant brand—the kind advertised on TV with video clips. The fat guy had bragged that his car could hit a hundred kilometers an hour in less than ten seconds. It was true: As soon as I stepped on the accelerator I easily pulled away from the other cars. Shame: so much motor for so little personality.

Insurgentes Avenue was deserted and ready for me to tear down the asphalt at two hundred kilometers an hour. I decided to drive slowly. I never liked speed. Neither did Gregorio. Not even in our high school days, when we'd borrow the cars of our female classmates' mothers, claiming it was due to serious emergencies, only to give them back two or three days later.

We both thought that at high speed life was subject to chance. We could be killed by another driver's recklessness, a stone in the middle of the road, or a crossing dog. Like our friend René (perhaps our only one), who was decapitated after his car drove under a trailer at a hundred and eighty kilometers an hour. The truck driver got distracted while peeling an orange and changed lanes just when René's car was overtaking him. René didn't have time to brake. His Golf was left with no roof—and no René—smashed against the door to an apartment building ninety yards away. René was in no hurry to get anywhere. He was going fast just because he wanted to.

I DROVE FOR SEVERAL BLOCKS without knowing where to go. I didn't want to go back home or to drive around town alone. And I certainly didn't plan on picking up the fat guy and his friends. They'd have enough fun looking for the car in the parking lot.

I was desperate for a pause. To stop and chat. Just chat. I wanted nothing else.

I headed toward Rebecca's house. There was a chance her boyfriend had left and I could see her for a while. It would be hard though—her parents were very strict and she had a curfew. Her family life was claustrophobic. Maybe that's why I liked my relationship with her; it gave me the feeling I was breaking something.

I'd only made love with Rebecca a few times. Twenty at most. All in unusual places: her parents' bedroom, the roof, her kitchen, the hallway of a lonely movie theater, an empty classroom. The reason: She refused to go to a motel. "They're for whores," she'd say.

She was sweet and impulsive, but predictable. She loved me very much and at some point I thought I was in love with her, too. It's probable that things would've been different had we ever been naked, calm, without our rushed caresses, without the danger of being caught with our pants around our knees, stuck to each other like stray dogs ready to have a bucket of cold water thrown on them. Different, if she hadn't been the daughter of a couple of conservative bastards. Different, especially, if I didn't love Tania so much.

I STOPPED IN FRONT of Rebecca's house. Her boyfriend's car was still parked in front of the door. I looked at the clock on the tape deck: twelve-seventeen. The boyfriend had exceeded the parents' limit by more than an hour and forty-five minutes. The father would kick him out any minute now.

I popped a cassette into the tape deck to endure the wait by listening to music, but the fat guy's taste was so poor I shut it off. I waited for ten minutes. Since the boyfriend wasn't leaving I decided to go to the corner to call Rebecca from a pay phone.

"Hello," she answered.

"Who is this?" I asked.

She got nervous and started to stammer. The agreement was that when I called her house I would ask for the imaginary Fernando Martinez. If we could talk without problems, the conversation would continue. If not, she would answer "I'm sorry, miss, you've got the wrong number" and hang up. As she started to say "wrong nu . . ." I interrupted her.

"Don't hang up," I ordered.

She remained silent.

"Don't hang up on me."

"This is 572–50–92," she said hesitantly.

On the other end of the phone I could hear her boyfriend asking who was calling.

"Do you miss me?" I asked her.

"Yes, miss."

"I want to see you right now."

"No, miss, I wish I could help you, but I don't think that's possible."

She covered the mouthpiece. Even so, I managed to hear her tell her boyfriend that a very distressed lady was trying to find the phone number for the Hospital de la Luz.

"What happened?" she asked disconcerted.

"Can you talk now?"

"Hurry, Antonio went to the kitchen to look for the phone book."

"I need to see you."

"Tomorrow."

"No, now."

"You're crazy."

She covered the phone again. She gave her boyfriend some instructions for where to find the phone book.

"He's gone again," she whispered.

"Good."

"Why haven't you been at school?"

"I haven't been able to."

"You stood me up last Wednesday. We were going to have lunch, remember? You didn't even call to apologize."

"I couldn't make it."

I could hear her boyfriend's voice in the background. Rebecca changed her tone of voice.

"Look, miss, the hospital phone number is . . ."

I interrupted her.

"Why don't you go walk your boyfriend?"

She continued in a neutral tone.

"You don't have anything to write with?"

"I'm on the corner of your block. When you leave to say good-bye to him, leave the door open and I'll sneak in."

"No, miss, I can't do that."

"I'll be waiting for you in a red car that's parked behind your boyfriend's."

"No, I can't wait while you get a pencil."

"Of course you can."

"Yes, yes, look: write this down. The number is five, four, zero . . ."

"I need to talk to you."

" . . .thirty-four . . ."

"Gregorio's dead."

Rebecca remained silent. I heard her breathe through her mouth.

" . . .eighty-one . . . and if I can I'll be happy to help you," she said and hung up.

FIVE MINUTES LATER the boyfriend appeared, sheathed in a raincoat. Rebecca, behind him, stood under a black umbrella. It started to drizzle. I sank into the seat when he walked past me toward his car. Rebecca caught up to him and gave him a kiss. From a window, her father shouted for her to hurry up. The boyfriend's car took off and Rebecca knocked her knuckles twice against my window. I sat up once the boyfriend's car turned the corner.

I got out of the car and, being careful not to make any noise, shut the door. Rebecca waited for me on the sidewalk. The father called out again.

"Hurry up and get inside."

"I'm coming," she answered.

Squatting, I moved three steps forward and leaned against the side. The old man was watching his daughter's movements from the window.

"What are you doing?" he asked with another shout.

"I dropped an earring and I'm looking for it."

Rebecca stood next to the door, turned toward her house and discreetly signaled for me to get in. Upon entering she gestured for me to hide behind a large clay pot at the edge of the garden. I heard the father's voice telling her to lock the front door.

Rebecca pretended to lock it several times.

"I'll be right back," she whispered.

The lights went off on the top floor. The only light left on was in a guest room next to the garden.

BETWEEN THE FRONT GATE and the house was a wide lawn hedged with gardenias, rosebushes, and cedars. To get to the main door I had to cross fifteen meters of a gravel path. The father was sure to booby trap it after midnight.

Several minutes went by. My legs became stiff and I got my hand covered in mud when, as I tried to shift positions, I stuck it in the pot.

The garden was lit by three powerful spotlights. You could clearly see the rain falling on the grass, the raindrops knocking the leaves off the trees and the blanket of bougainvillea flowers spread over the floor. Dozens of earthworms writhed on the gravel, fleeing their flooded holes. A couple of rats stealthily crossed the lawn, climbed onto the garbage cans in the garage, rummaged for scraps of food and scuttled back into a crack under the disused fountain.

Rebecca, dressed only in a black satin nightgown and shawl, came out to find me. She hissed from the front door. I got up, my back aching. I cleaned the mud off the soles of my shoes with a rock and went down the dimmer side of the path.

Once I climbed the stairs to the entrance, Rebecca hugged me and kissed me. Her cheek was warm. So were her lips. She grabbed me by the left hand and stealthily led me through the darkened living room.

"If my dad finds you here, he'll kill you."

"We'll kill each other."

She smiled and shook her head. Her hair moved like Tania's.

"My dad's not as bad as he looks."

"Of course not; he's worse."

She punched me in the stomach. I pretended she'd knocked the wind out of me. She noticed my dirty hand. She showed me a bathroom in the same room.

"Do you always wear that nightgown, or did you wear it for me?" I asked, looking at her through the mirror as I washed my hands.

"It's the one I wear every night thinking of you."

She took off the shawl and sat on a sofa. The skin on her shoulders was smooth and white—a white that wasn't unpleasant.

I finished drying my hands, took my jacket off, and sat down next to her.

"Is it true, what you said on the phone?" she asked.

"Yes."

She'd only met Gregorio twice—enough to know how intimidating he was. When she met him, Rebecca was wearing a blouse that showed her shoulders. Gregorio stroked them, barely touching them with the tips of his fingers. She pulled away, startled. "I just wanted to know if they were real," he said.

"What did he die of?"

Gregorio had died of so many things that I refused to say the word *suicide.*

"He's dead. Period," I said.

She wasn't bothered by my answer. She opened my hand and ran her index finger over the lines in my palm. She made no absurd predictions about my future or the probable length of my life. She only traced "M" over and over.

"I got very nervous when you called," she said.

"You thought your boyfriend would find out?" I asked.

She kissed the palm of my hand and let it go.

"No, I don't care about that. I was nervous it was you."

She lay down and put her head on my lap.

"Last Wednesday, when you stood me up, I was afraid."

"Of what?"

"That you didn't want to see me anymore."

I leaned over and kissed her forehead. She was frequently afraid that I'd abandon her under some pretext.

"Don't be silly," I said.

We heard footsteps upstairs. Rebecca sat up and tilted her head, trying to identify the source of the noise.

"It's Sancho," she said, relieved.

Sancho was the dog—a midget mutt that, despite being some godforsaken breed, didn't irritate everyone by barking at anything that moved.

Rebecca lay down on my legs again.

"When did Gregorio die?"

"Tuesday afternoon. That's why I didn't make it on Wednesday."

"Forget Wednesday," she said and kissed me.

It was getting harder to talk about Gregorio.

"When did they bury him?"

I couldn't answer. Sancho sniffed under the door. He scratched a bit, then walked away.

"Were you able to see him before he died?"

I nodded.

"Did you make peace?"

How to explain to her that it wasn't about fixing misunderstandings or working out discord among friends. This wasn't about making peace, it was about forgiving each other. When would we be able to forgive each other now?

I felt a sudden desire to cry, to appear fragile before the girl with the white shoulders, to run and squeeze just one last word out of Gregorio's ashes.

Rebecca looked at me, unable to understand. She wrapped herself around my waist and, like that, not knowing why, cried for me.

THE RAIN STOPPED. One, then two still hours went by and we didn't talk. She had slipped off the straps to her nightgown. Her breasts emerged. They were as white as her shoulders. I traced circles around her erect nipples with my finger. With no hurry, no desire.

She kissed me and undressed. Still clothed, I fell asleep on her pubis. I woke up when she moved.

"My leg's getting a cramp," she said, smiling.

"Sorry," I said and bit the thin fold on her belly.

I sat up and she ran her fingers through my hair. I hugged her naked body.

"I can't believe you're still here and my parents are sleeping upstairs. We're so cynical."

"No, no we're not."

She pulled away from me and threw her head back.

"You know what?" she asked.

"Mmmmhh."

"I'm in love with you."

She sighed and put my hand on her chest.

"Feel it," she said.

I lowered my hand slowly over her nakedness. When I reached her inner thigh she caught my hand between her legs.

"I can't love you this much anymore," she whispered. "I love you too much."

She looked me in the eyes and bit her lips.

"I can't see you anymore," she said.

"Why?"

She kissed me on the mouth and rubbed the scent of her naked body over mine.

"I can't," she mumbled, "really, I can't."

She pulled away from me, got dressed, covered herself with the shawl, and went up the stairs to her room.

I WALKED OUT into the garden. A soft fog stretched over the top of the trees. Drops of water drummed irregularly on the window ledges and the grass emanated thick humidity.

From among the shadows, a black butterfly emerged. It crossed through the beams of the spotlights and flew back into the night. When I was little I used to collect ones like that. I'd catch them by the tip of their wings and run a needle through them onto a piece of cardboard where they'd die desperately flapping.

Sancho peeked through the half-open door and sat down next to me to watch the garden. From his collar hung a metal tag with his name, address, and Rebecca's phone number. I squatted, patted him on the back, grabbed the chain, and twisted the tag off. I squeezed it in my hand and then put it in my pocket.

I lifted Sancho, put him on the entrance hall floor and closed the door.

Rebecca and I never made love again.

THE FAT GUY'S car alarm triggered when I opened the door. I pressed the buttons on the remote in every combination possible before I managed to deactivate it. I didn't remember turning it on.

I started the car. The tape deck indicated it was four-seventeen AM. I put my seat belt on and drove home.

I didn't find anyone with whom to leave the car. There was only a mess of amber-colored glass on the courts. I searched through the glove compartment to find out where the fat guy lived from his registration. He lived twelve blocks down, at the bottom of the hill.

"Fuck," I thought, "now I have to walk back uphill."

I parked the car in front of Pino Street and dropped the keys in the mailbox. They hit the bottom with a metallic clang and I walked away in a hurry.

IN THE KITCHEN, my mother had left another plate of sandwiches, this time without onion. Next to them was a note: "Manuel, I hope you like these ones. Love, your mom."

My mother always felt guilty when she worked, thinking

that we believed she neglected her children, abandoning us for her career. She lived a half-life, neither fully finding herself in one place nor the other. "I'm only good at doing one thing at a time," I once heard her tell my father when they were arguing. In the end, in the pendulum of her choices, Luis and I would always end up losing. She was never with us, even when she was.

I sat down to eat the same sandwiches I'd had my entire life: two slices of toasted bread, coated with a layer of mayonnaise, a little mustard, and stuffed full of shredded chicken. Sometimes they had lettuce, pickles, tomato, and, frequently, onions.

They are lodged in my memory in little plastic bags in my lunch box at recess. They were the only food at picnics and the main course at parties. Breakfasts, lunches, dinners. Sandwiches and more sandwiches. I don't hate them like Luis does. On the contrary, when I travel, I miss them. I miss their flat, familiar taste, probably as much as I miss my home.

I TOOK MY MESSAGE book and went over all that had accumulated over the course of two years. Slices of my past compiled in who called, at what time, and for what reason. My past.

Among the dozens of calls Gregorio had made, two stuck out. The first was one he had made from the hospital on the first of October, a year and a half ago. He was making use of the one phone call he was allowed that week (three minutes, no more, every seven days). The message was concise: "No war." Just like that.

"No war over this whore," Gregorio had said days earlier in the hospital when I finally had had the courage to confess— more like confirm—my relationship with Tania. He seemed to have prepared the phrase just to say it at that moment.

"We're above this, right?" he said calmly.

"We are," I answered.

He looked calm, with that calmness only attained with high doses of sedatives. He drew close to my ear.

"There's no war."

The male nurses grabbed him by the shoulders and pulled him back.

"I believe you," I said.

He clicked his tongue.

"No, you don't."

He was right: I didn't believe him. A doctor came into the cubicle and ended the visit.

"No war," he said in parting.

He retired (to his room? his cell? his what?) followed closely by the nurses. He went back to the shock therapy sessions, to the padded walls, to the mornings of syringes and pills, to the three-minute phone calls every 168 hours, to the evenings without Tania, to the barred landscape, to the hallways lit 24 hours a day, to fending off the flurries of his psychosis alone.

Gregorio's other noticeable phone call in my message book was written down by my brother on the twenty-second of February at four-seventeen in the afternoon. Gregorio had left no message, even though two hours later, with a bullet, he left us all one.

I tore out the sheets corresponding to October first and February the twenty-second from my message book. I folded them and put them in a pocket in my wallet.

I WALKED INTO my room, taking care not to make any noise. I undressed. I could still feel Rebecca's pubic hair on my face, her breath, her scent. I missed her.

She decided to leave me before she lost me. At the time it made no sense. Now I see why.

I brushed my teeth, rinsed my face and shaved. When I walked out of the bathroom, I found my father sitting on my bed.

"How'd it go?" he asked.

"Fine."

"You should've let us know where you were going."

"I didn't know. I was just around."

With his hand, he invited me to sit down next to him.

"Tania's mom called."

"And?"

"They know where she is."

It weighed on me that they should have found her before I did.

"Since the day before yesterday she's been staying at a friend's house, Mónica Abín. You know her?"

"Yes."

"Her parents are going to go pick her up at eight-thirty."

I looked at the alarm clock and he smiled.

"That's in three hours," he said.

I smiled, too. It would be dawn any minute now.

"How is she?"

"Fine, I guess."

He stood up and drew an oval with his index finger on my forehead. He used to do that to soothe me when I was awakened by nightmares when I was little.

"Are you going to go see her?"

I didn't answer.

"Go to sleep, it's late," he ordered.

He walked toward the door and stopped at the threshold.

"Should I turn the light off?"

I nodded.

"Good night," he said.

The room was dark. I heard his footsteps walking down the hall. I wrapped myself in the blankets and cried.

I WAS AWAKENED by the noise of a car. I didn't know if it was morning or evening. I rubbed my eyes and got up. The alarm clock showed it was five-twenty. I'd slept for almost twelve hours, and the first three were restless. I woke up shaking two or three times: Again, I'd felt the breathing of the dark beast. Again, close, spectral, furious.

Nevertheless, I awoke relaxed. My last dream had been peaceful. Gregorio and I were thirteen years old. We were watching Tania play volleyball in the central schoolyard. She and her friends were still little girls. They could barely control the ball and send it over the net. Alarid, the P.E. teacher, whistled and corrected their technique from a distance. Tania laughed, amused. She knew she was being watched, floating above the others, as usual.

When the game ended, the crowd around the court began to scatter. Friends from secondary school walked past me, friends I had loved very much and had never heard from again: Nayeli Osio, who I loved like a sister; Denisse Cooley; Sonia Aranda; Rafael Hernández; James Zapata; Joel; Carlos; George; Rosa Silva; Mónica Márquez; Giselle; Gina; Ada; Rosa María Butchfield; Gaby Ricoy. I was happy to see them. I wanted to ask them how they were doing, what had become of them, but I didn't dare speak to them. Neither did Gregorio. They walked lost in thought. Only Tania looked at us.

• • •

I GOT UP TO LOOK for my secondary school class photograph.
I found it forgotten in a corner of the closet, under some football
shoes and boxing gloves. I blew the dust off of it. We were all
sitting there, living in other bodies, other faces, other gestures.
Tania was sitting in the middle of the first row, with the sleeves
of her sweater rolled up, slightly turning her face, looking at the
photographer, not the camera. Above, Gregorio looking without
looking, foreign to the act. I was standing next to him with my
right fist clenched, my hair over my eyes, without smiling.

Did the rest of the group know Gregorio was dead? Did Mónica
Márquez know, who once slapped him? Carlos Samaniego, who
offered Gregorio a lime popsicle that he was too shy to accept?
Vera, who lent him her math notes? Luis García Kobeh, who invited him on vacation to Valle de Bravo for a weekend? Did they
know? Would they care?

Many of them ended up afraid of him, others seduced. The
rest were confused. In secondary school, Gregorio didn't show
any signs of what was to come. Nobody, not even I could pre-
dict that. Who could guess that that withdrawn boy would turn
so suddenly to the extreme. Who could explain what drove him
to that separate reality? Who?

I OPENED THE CURTAINS. The afternoon was clear, with a brilliant sun, although a mass of gray clouds was approaching from
the north. "Cumulus congestus" with the tendency to form "cu-
mulonimbus." Certain to become a tempest according to what
Jaime A. Bastos, my geography teacher (one of the few real
teachers I ever had), explained in class. He would combine

quotes from Shakespeare with methods—scientific and intuitive—for predicting rain.

My mother had slid a note with messages for me under the door. Margarita had called twice and asked that I should call her as soon as possible. Doctor Macías also called. Again, he had left a series of telephone numbers where I could reach him.

"PSYCHOTIC EPISODE" was the term Doctor Macías first used to describe Gregorio's sudden change in personality. He predicted a medium term recovery and asked friends and family for patience and support. He explained that Gregorio's life would oscillate between periods of normality and occasional relapses, though he never told the parents how often or serious these relapses would be. He never told them what they would be facing.

When Gregorio's "sane" days became increasingly scarce, Macías tried to conceal the snowballing madness in ambiguous psychiatric jargon: schizophrenia, paranoid delusions, bipolar traits, blah, blah, blah. Every meeting with the parents he'd offer a new hypothesis, driving them even further into confusion and despair.

FOUR MONTHS before the suicide, Macías and his team of doctors claimed that Gregorio was progressing toward a full rehabilitation and that he could soon return to normal life. They gradually reduced his periods of isolation, his medication, and the corrective measures. Until they finally released him. They didn't realize that Gregorio had learned to fake the signs of improvement they rewarded: the easy, affectionate smile; the fluent chatter; the measured gestures; the attentive gaze; the relaxed demeanor. Cracked on the inside, he knew how to project his chameleon charm and, believe it or not, he tricked them.

They let him go despite his mother's resistance—she knew her son's change to be fake. The psychiatrists insisted the improvements were real and sustained. Besides, they offered close and continuous supervision. "Don't worry," Macías concluded, "your son is on the right track."

So, Gregorio rid himself of the endless hospital lighting, of the nurses who forcefully subdued him, of the stupefying drugs. He was free to pour his destructive fury upon himself.

And he won by defeating himself.

I WALKED OUT of the room and didn't see my parents. They had left a note saying they'd gone to the supermarket and would be back in the evening.

I took Gregorio's box out of the closet. It made me nervous: The task of looking through its contents overwhelmed me. It meant facing the last chronicle of his madness and maybe even unraveling the motives that led him to kill himself in his bathroom on precisely the twenty-second of February at six-seventeen PM.

It was clear Gregorio foresaw that Margarita wouldn't dare open the box. He'd delivered it to her so it would reach someone else. She was a courier. I can bet it was for Tania or myself.

I lifted the cover off the box. On top was the envelope with the photographs. There were twenty-two, taken with a little instamatic. They were color prints—some blurry, some overexposed. All recent. Gregorio appeared next to the nurses and doctors in the gardens and patios of the psychiatric hospital. Smiling faces predominated and it seemed they were celebrating Gregorio's departure.

I noticed that in twelve of the photos, Gregorio appeared next to a patient dressed in a blue gown: a man reaching his thirties whom I didn't know. He was a redhead, with long curly hair, tall, robust, with a soft gaze. Their arms were around each other's shoulders as if they were great friends.

I PUT THE PHOTOGRAPHS down. There were four packets in the box, each tied with a different-colored ribbon: green, blue, red, and black. The choice of colors wasn't arbitrary. There must be some intention, a premeditated order. Which packet to open first?

The black one didn't mean death and the red one didn't mean blood. No, Gregorio's clues weren't that obvious. The package with the most dangerous content would've been green, since it's a neutral color, or blue, because it represented the buffalo's breath (there was a reason why Gregorio insisted we get tattoos with blue ink).

My suspicions seemed fanciful and paranoid. What was the point in assigning Gregorio postmortem intentions? Again, I thought of closing the box and throwing it away. Besides, why begin a game with an adversary literally reduced to ashes? But what if the box really did contain some form of defiance?

Tania was right: Gregorio hadn't finished dying yet.

I STARTED BY OPENING the package with the black ribbon. There was a folded napkin on top. I unfolded it and spread it on the bed. Written on it were two phrases from a vacuous pop song: "Near you, everything is new / it's being in the fire's center."

Gregorio hadn't written them. It didn't look like a woman's

handwriting either. It was an indefinite hand, without personality.

Next came a squared piece of paper, torn from an accounting book. It also had ballad verses copied in the same mediocre calligraphy: "I feel you in my heart, / fiery blood, / slow flow / of your endless love."

In the same way, I found several pieces of paper until I came upon an oval portrait, credential-size, in black and white—the kind used in official documents. Despite the fact that the face was thin and adolescent, it wasn't hard for me to recognize the redhead from the photographs.

Behind the portrait was written, in the same dull script, a name and a date: Jacinto Anaya, June 17, 1980.

Everything indicated that it was he who had copied down the cheesy lyrics of lost love, idyllic reconciliations, kisses on the beach. Why had Gregorio kept them? I doubted the possibility of Gregorio being gay. Gregorio was homophobic. What, then?

I COUNTED A TOTAL of seventeen pieces of paper with lyrics on them. For an hour and a half I moved them around trying to solve the possibility of a crossword puzzle. Nothing—the phrases didn't fit together. I separated the words and made them into new sentences in search of some more coherent plot. Again, nothing.

I wound up with a headache, without being able to clear up any of the hidden allegories. I called Margarita to ask her if she knew what they meant. Nobody answered.

My parents arrived and a few minutes later my mother knocked on my door. They'd brought some pastries and she asked if I wanted to have dinner with them.

We sat at the kitchen table. My father and I at either end. My mother in the middle. There was an assortment of bread and pastry: croissants, doughnuts, a bear claw. They didn't bring my favorite: Danish. My father apologized and said that he didn't know if I was going to have dinner with them. I missed the nights when they bought me Danish, whether they knew if I was going to have dinner with them or not.

My father talked about some problems at work. He was sick of one of his coworkers, fat and ugly, who had the habit of piecing her life out of the fragments of others. She sat at her desk to eavesdrop on other people's conversations, register who went in or out of which office, and make up love affairs where they didn't exist. My mother pointed out that there was nothing to worry about. "There are plenty of women like that," she said. "They're almost part of the furniture." We laughed and then grew quiet.

From the house next door came loud music. My father complained. It was the same thing every weekend: music and noise that kept him from sleeping. The culprit was Vanessa, the neighbors' daughter, a girl who threw high school parties every Saturday night.

In other circumstances I would've complained to my father, but I remained silent to listen to the words of the song they were playing. I didn't pick up any of the phrases copied by Jacinto Anaya.

My father pounded on the wall with his fist. It was part of the Saturday ritual. The girl lowered the volume, but ten minutes later turned it up again.

"When is she going to learn?" my father lamented.

"When she gets a boyfriend," answered my mother.

True: Vanessa needed someone to unbutton her blouse and stroke the lumps under her bra. Only then would she be quiet.

. . .

THE PHONE RANG. My mother answered and, covering the receiver, whispered that it was Doctor Macías. I signaled for her to say I wasn't there. She signaled that she wouldn't. Annoyed, I grabbed the phone.

It was Macías himself, not the secretary. In his treble voice he asked me to go see him. "I can't this week, I've got exams," I explained. "This is urgent," he insisted. I said I'd meet him in his office on Monday at six PM.

"I can understand that you don't want to go to the hospital," he said in his pedantic, paternal tone, supposing that the hospital would bring me painful memories. Actually, I preferred his office because it was closer to my house, even though I didn't plan on going anyway.

I'D SEEN HIM on three separate occasions. The first time he called me into his assistant director's office at the psychiatric hospital. After making me wait for two hours he let me in and asked me to sit down in a chair upholstered with black leather. He remained standing, looked at me over his glasses, and in five minutes—as if he were a tour guide running through his usual routine—he explained that to help Gregorio it was first necessary to help ourselves. He suggested I start therapy "which any of our specialists will gladly provide at a low cost." He said the same thing to Joaquín, Margarita, and Tania.

The second time, I ran into him in one of the hospital gardens. We walked together for a stretch and then Macías stopped. He started an affable chat that turned into an aggressive inquiry: What's your relationship with Gregorio? How does he treat his parents? What does he say about the hospital? How does he feel?

From his attitude, it was perfectly clear that Gregorio was winning the doctor/patient chess game, and that Macías was gathering whatever information he could in order to face him.

I made up most of my answers, but took care to make them believable. With each one Macías nodded gravely. "Now I understand," "clearly," "Yes, I thought so."

His last question focused on Gregorio's earwig obsession. This time I told him the truth. It was the only answer Macías didn't believe.

The third and last time I met with him was at his office. He received me suspiciously. He considered me to be one of Gregorio's allies, bent on sabotaging his work as a psychiatrist, someone to be treated with severity.

For half an hour he lectured me on the importance of collaborating with the doctors in the patient's rehabilitation. "It's you, his friends, who must stand by and watch over him when he leaves the hospital," he said eloquently. Several times he emphasized the phrase "we have to anchor him" (a phrase that wouldn't sound that bad in a pop song: "our love, we've got to anchor it, day and night, we've got to anchor it"). When I asked what we had to anchor him to, Macías gazed at me harshly. "Let's try not to be clever," he mumbled, through a forced smile.

Every time I encountered him, I tried to cover the remains of the blue buffalo. I didn't want him to ask me any more questions than he had to.

DURING SECONDARY SCHOOL I protected and took care of Gregorio. Quiet and withdrawn as he was, lots of kids enjoyed harassing him. He would never put up a fight, and allowed himself to be humiliated. The abuse infuriated me and on multiple occasions I fought for him. I usually lost. Gregorio was the amusement of many, and among many they'd beat the shit out of me.

Gregorio would get good grades without having to study much. The professors appreciated him, though few of them were aware of him. "He's invisible," I once heard the math professor say. "You don't notice him, you don't sense him, and I only know he exists when I check attendance."

Three years of secondary school went by like this and almost the entire first year of high school. It was in those last months when the furious and irreversible change overcame him. It all started in chemistry class, with the teacher asking a pointless question: "Which acid makes chiles spicy?" From the back of the room came Gregorio's answer: "Chilehydric acid." Some kids giggled. Arrogant, Gregorio repeated his joke. The teacher just stared at him in disbelief. Gregorio had never behaved like this. As a reprimand, the teacher took two points off his monthly grade and gave him a demerit mark on the much-feared report sheet, which the janitor usually picked up at the end of the day and took to the principal's office. Two demerit marks meant a three-day suspension.

At the end of the class, the teacher left the report on his desk, where no student could take it without risking expulsion from school for an entire week. As soon as the teacher left, Gregorio grabbed the piece of paper, tore it into small pieces, and sprinkled it over the desks like confetti. The other kids thought it was stupid—a mama's boy throwing a tantrum.

In the evening I stopped by his house, still surprised by his rebelliousness. He welcomed me, proud. When I asked him why he'd done it, he showed me his left middle finger. There was a purple line under his nail.

"What happened?" I asked.

He drew close. In a low voice he made me promise I'd keep the secret.

"An earwig crawled up there."

He explained the earwig had run through his arteries and widened them.

"Now, more blood flows to my brain," he said joyfully, "more oxygen, more light . . ."

I laughed thinking he was making a joke, but he would never be the same.

I told all this to Dr. Macías and he didn't believe me.

AFTER DINNER I went up to my room. I put the packets back in order and hid the box in the closet. Enough riddles for the day.

Outside the window I observed a succession of lightning bolts prefacing a tempest. The sky was darker than usual. They say nights get this black before an earthquake.

It was barely nine o'clock and I was neither tired nor had any desire to go out. I didn't particularly want a night of ennui, watching Spanish game shows or sensationalist newscasts, but I couldn't come up with a way of avoiding the tedium.

I wanted to call Tania, but I stopped myself. She needed time to heal her wounds in her own way. There was no need to pressure her. She'd come back; she always did.

I turned on the radio and listened, station after station, trying to find some of the phrases jotted down by Jacinto Anaya. Maybe by listening to the ballads in their entirety I could piece together the meaning of what Gregorio was trying to say.

• • •

IT STARTED TO HAIL and I turned off the radio. The roof and walls resounded. The windows seemed to crack with every impact and the rattle of ice marbles against the bathroom skylight made a thick, deafening racket. I looked into the street. The pavement was instantly covered in white. The cars advanced cautiously and the gaps left by the tires were quickly filled with a new layer of hail. To my left, in the distance, I spotted an old man huddling against the wall of an abandoned lot for shelter.

For a while, the electric light fluctuated. The bulbs flickered weakly and the light in the room acquired an amber shade, similar to the light emitted by a small lamp my mother used to leave on at night when Luis and I were little. An enveloping, warm light that made me feel good.

The hailstorm passed and left a quiet, thin rain. You could only hear the branches scratching against the walls when the wind picked up.

After several minutes the voltage steadied and the light of my childhood dissipated. Soon after that my mother knocked on the door to tell me Margarita was on the phone. I connected the phone in my room and answered.

"Hello."

Margarita didn't answer. She seemed distracted.

"Hello," I repeated.

"Why didn't you call me earlier?" she demanded.

Even though her reproach annoyed me, I tried to explain myself.

"I dialed twice, but no—"

She interrupted me. "Tania's car has been parked outside my house for three hours."

"What?"

"She's been locked in there the entire time. She did the same thing yesterday."

"Are you sure?"

"I'm looking at her from my window right now."

I was disturbed. I had imagined Tania at home, relaxed, beside her parents. Margarita said that she had tried to go talk to her twice already, but that Tania had driven away only to return twenty or thirty minutes later.

"She's just been sitting there, staring out the windshield," she added.

I decided to go look for her. I got dressed, put on a thick sweater, and asked my father to lend me his car. He gave me the keys without asking questions.

I DROVE FULL SPEED. The drizzle still hadn't let up. Piles of hail had accumulated on the sidewalk. The streets were filthy with mud, branches, and leaves. A bottleneck formed at the crossroads between Periferico and Barranca del Muerto. I avoided it by driving up onto the sidewalk for a stretch, before the indolent stare of two traffic cops.

I arrived and parked half a block away from Gregorio's house. It was better to approach on foot, cautiously, so Tania wouldn't drive away when she saw me.

I found her leaning on the steering wheel. Her hair fell to one side, covering her face. I knocked on the window with a coin. She turned slowly and looked at me through the foggy glass. I thought she'd leave. She lowered the window a few centimeters and stuck out two fingers. I took them in my hand.

"You're cold, get in," she said.

She unlocked the doors and I walked around. Against the light, I noticed Margarita's silhouette peeking through the window. With a slight nod I let her know that everything was okay.

I opened the door and got in. The inside of the car was warm, comfortable. I could smell a trace of cigarette smoke. Tania stretched out her arm and turned off the CD player. She then placed her hand on the seat, opened it, and I took it in mine.

She looked me in the eyes. She seemed tired but composed. It didn't look as if she'd been crying.

"How did you know I was here?"

"This was the last place I was going to check."

She squeezed my hand and deeply breathed in.

"I was looking for you, too," she said.

I pulled her toward me and hugged her. Docile, she nestled into my chest. I kissed the nape of her neck.

"So, what are you doing here?" I asked.

"Waiting for you to come."

She lifted her face and kissed me on the mouth. A car turned into the street and its headlights shone directly on us. Tania pulled away from me and watched the car drive away.

"That's the third one in an hour," she said with a smile.

She kissed me again. Her kisses weren't tense; they were sweet, relaxed.

"I missed you," she said and hugged me.

Upon doing so, her blouse lifted and a fringe of her waist was left bare. I touched her with my right index finger. Her skin bristled.

"You're freezing," she said.

I untucked the rest of her blouse and put my hand on her stomach. She moaned softly. I felt the measure of her breath, her heartbeat, her warm skin cooling against mine.

"Manuel, you're freezing, get your hand out of there."

I pressed against her belly. It contracted.

"Out," she mumbled.

I lowered my hand and quickly slipped it into her pants. I brushed against her pubic hair with the tips of my fingers.

Tania straightened up and looked me in the eyes again.

"Please, Manuel, get it out."

I pulled my hand out. My fingers kept the trace of her warmth and the pulse of her body. Her eyes misted over but she still stared at me fixedly.

"Where were you?" I asked.

She didn't answer. She frowned slightly.

"Where?" I insisted.

With the back of her hand she stroked my cheek and then ran it over the bridge of my nose. I slowly pulled back. Her hand was left in the air. She turned her face and looked ahead. The windshield was riddled with raindrops. Tania turned the windshield wipers to half speed and followed the motions of the rubber on the glass with her eyes.

I turned the keys and pulled them out of the ignition. The windshield wipers stopped midway.

"You can tell me."

Tania lowered her head and sighed.

"I was around."

"Why?"

"I don't know."

We remained silent, apart. Our breaths fogged the windows. We heard the steps of someone running down the sidewalk but we couldn't see him. Tania held out her left arm and showed me the watch on her wrist: ten-thirty. It was a watch Gregorio had given her for Christmas once.

"I have to go," she said. "It's late and I told my parents I'd be back before ten-thirty."

"You disappear for days and now you're worried about getting home by ten-thirty? Call them and tell them you'll be home later."

"I can't."

"You did for two nights in a row, I don't see why you can't for a third."

No matter how much I insisted, she refused. She also wouldn't let me escort her home. I gave her back the keys to her car.

"Are you sure?"

She nodded. I opened the door.

"Do you know?" she asked before I stepped out. In our good-byes, this meant "You know how much I love you, right?" I was supposed to answer: "Yes, I know," securely, like I used to night after night.

"No, I don't," I answered. It hurt me to say it, but I really didn't.

She looked me in the eyes (her gaze, always her gaze).

"You should know," she said, "because I love you more than ever."

"By hiding?"

She bit her lips, slid her fingers under my shirtsleeve and stroked my wrist.

"Yes, by hiding."

I tried to get out of the car but she held me by my elbow.

"I'm getting wet," I said.

Her eyes grew misty again.

"I'm hiding from myself, not you," she whispered. She barely kissed me on the lips and pulled away.

"I'll see you tomorrow," she said.

She drove away and her car got lost in the rainy night.

· · ·

I STOOD UNDER THE WINDOW to Margarita's room and threw some stones at it. She opened the window and looked out.

"D'you want to come in?" she asked.

I shook my head.

"What, then?"

"Come."

She looked at me, puzzled. I had said "come" in the same secretive tone as before.

"Come," I insisted.

Margarita watched me, indecisive.

"Wait," she said.

I went to get the car and parked it by the sidewalk next to her house. On our previous clandestine encounters, Margarita used to sneak out through a door that led to the garden, but this time she walked out the front.

She walked out in tight gray sweatpants, protected by a red umbrella. Her irregular body stood out under the cotton fabric: wide hips, flat ass, long legs, big tits. It was a body I had always liked, without any perfection to ruin it.

I honked the horn and Margarita ran to the car.

"What happened?" she asked.

"Nothing."

She opened the window and shook the umbrella.

"Where are we going?" she asked.

I shrugged my shoulders.

"I don't know."

"Okay," she sighed.

WE DROVE AIMLESSLY around the city. I briefly told her about my meeting with Tania. She listened without interrupting.

When I finished, we remained silent and didn't speak for the rest of the trip.

Even though we had promised never to sleep together again, that night we ended up at the entrance to a motel on the Toluca highway. When the man who led us to the room asked us to pay, we had to leave. Neither of us had enough money.

I thought of taking her to room 803, but I didn't dare. I even felt guilty. It was like soiling my marriage bed, my most private space.

We kept driving around, not knowing where to go. Turned on, she started to lick my ear and I started to grope her inner thigh. I stopped at a pharmacy to buy condoms. I barely scraped enough together to pay for them.

I drove all the way to one of the desolate projects to which I used to go with Tania, and we parked on a dark, lonely street. We hurriedly kissed. I slipped on the condom and she pulled her sweatpants down to her knees. She turned her back to me and I tried to penetrate her. I couldn't. She pulled herself up with the dashboard and straightened out so I could put it in with more ease, but she slipped and fell on my thighs. Anxious, I told her to take her clothes off. She did. I licked her breasts and her stomach. I straddled her over my legs and held her by her armpits. We were both sweating. She pushed her pubis forward, but when I was about to enter her we both held back. We looked at each other. She dismounted, breathing heavily, and kneeled on the seat. She leaned over, took my cock in her left hand, pulled the condom off, and sucked it delicately for a few seconds. Then she kissed it good-bye, got up and sat down. She made no effort to get dressed. She pensively sat there with her legs open. She leaned on the seatback and rubbed her forehead in circles. Her nakedness was touching. I leaned my head and stroked her shoulder. I wanted to say I was sorry, even though there was no reason to.

A watchman at a nearby construction site walked out in a gray raincoat. He looked at our car from a distance. Margarita didn't try to cover herself. She just turned her torso and leaned against the seat.

The watchman went back to the construction site. Again, Margarita sat back with her legs open.

"Do you want us to give it another shot?" she asked.

"No."

The fourth or fifth time we had sex was under similar conditions: in a borrowed car, parked at the edge of a dusty soccer field on a hot April morning. Back then we were distanced by the gratuitous panting, the stuffy smell, the clothes stained by our secretions, and, especially, the violent absence of words after our orgasms.

That rainy Saturday, despite wanting her more than ever, I preferred to have her calmly sit naked beside me. I wanted her more as a friend than a lover. It was hard for me to touch her. Only seven days before, I'd seen Gregorio for the last time, and the impressions of his words and his last hug still bristled inside me. That hug was prolonged in Margarita's gaze and gestures.

I looked at her breasts, barely visible in the darkness. They'd lost their poise only to collapse, inert, on the folds of her belly. They were now soft, almost maternal breasts. Maternal: Margarita frequently looked after me. She helped my relationship with Tania flourish. She helped arrange our dates, make up excuses. She served as an alibi without caring that the person we were cheating on was her brother.

We came to be so close, so complicit, that one afternoon, unexpectedly, we ended up in her bed while her mother was having a nap in the next room and Gregorio was enduring his second lockup. It was a quickie, inexplicable, which we both decided to repeat whenever we could.

Lies on lies on lies.

MARGARITA WAS A WOMAN who easily orgasmed, with no need for sappy caresses or prefabricated phrases. She was simple and carnal, willing to offer her body without hesitation or the need to dole out guilt.

She kept our relationship to herself. She knew how to keep a secret and be discreet. She even knew how to keep quiet when she found Gregorio and me lying on her kitchen floor. He, with a torn chest. Me, with a sliced thigh. Both with the knives still hot in our hands.

She walked in and was struck dumb, unable to decipher the jigsaw puzzle of blood and broken glass she found scattered over the floor. She didn't lose her cool; she didn't scream. She picked up the phone and called an ambulance. Then she evaluated which of us was in more urgent need of medical attention. She decided it was Gregorio. She helped him up, led him out, and drove him to the hospital.

The ambulance came for me a few minutes later. I claimed it was an accident, that I'd tripped and fallen through the kitchen window. I got stitches at the Red Cross and my parents came to get me. I never told them the cause of my injury. Gregorio didn't tell his parents either. And Margarita knew how to keep quiet.

Margarita remained silent, sitting with her legs open. She shivered from the cold and grabbed her arms for warmth. She asked me to turn the radio on. "La Macarena" was playing and she started to move her body to the rhythm. Her soft breasts jiggled.

I held them with my right hand and felt their contours. She grabbed them with her own hands and lifted them.

"When I'm fifty they'll be hanging down to my belly button," she said and laughed.

I stared at her breasts until I suddenly realized she was crying. It was the first time I'd ever seen her cry. Her weeping was more inward than outward. I tried to hug her but she pushed me away and covered her face.

"Don't look at me, goddammit!"

I turned off the radio. Margarita doubled over her thighs. Her clean and naked back shook lightly with every sob. Again, I tried to console her and she rejected me.

I decided to let her calm down alone. I got out of the car. It had stopped raining. The air was cold. In the distance, the lights trembled on the skirts of Mount Ajusco.

Stealthily, the watchman appeared by the side of the construction site and walked into the middle of the street.

"'Evening," I said.

"'Evening," he muttered.

I walked toward him. He waited with a grim face, his hands in his raincoat, probably clutching a rusty revolver.

"It's getting cold, isn't it . . ." I said in an effort to make conversation.

He nodded without looking at me. A stray dog walked out of the site, sniffed me, and went to pee on a nearby post. In one of the rooms on the ground floor, the embers of a fire glowed. I asked the man for a cigarette. He pulled out a pack of cheap, unfiltered cigarettes and offered me one. I asked him if he had a light and he pointed at the fire in the house. I lit the cigarette with a half-burned branch. I coughed when I inhaled. I didn't usually smoke, but that night I thought I needed it to get rid of the cold.

I walked back to the watchman. A bat squeaked over our heads and flew away. I tried to see it in the darkness. The man observed each of my movements, looking out of the corner of his eye. I took a few steps and we were face-to-face.

"Why are you here?" he asked.

I pointed at the car.

"Just to be with my girlfriend for a while."

He looked at me skeptically.

"That's it?"

"That's it."

Without another word, he went back into the half-built house and lay down on a cot next to the fire. The dog followed and lay down next to him. The man wrapped himself in a blanket and turned his back to me.

I RETURNED TO THE CAR. I took three drags off the cigarette and flicked it into a puddle. Margarita had gotten dressed. She looked calmer, but fragile. I had never felt the urge to protect her before. I was anxious to guard her, mostly from myself.

She smiled sadly at me. I took her by the nape of her neck, pulled her toward me, and kissed her on the mouth.

"I'm sorry," she said when we separated.

"Why? What are you sorry about?"

"I don't know," she mumbled.

We drove away and left the watchman and his dog behind. It started to clear up, and a luminous half-moon appeared in the sky.

"The Turkish moon," Margarita said.

"Pisces moon," I added.

Margarita turned on the radio. In the song that came on, I noticed some of the lyrics that Jacinto Anaya had jotted down. It was a truly sappy ballad. Margarita moved to change the station.

"Leave it on," I ordered.

I turned up the volume.

"What are you doing?" she asked.

I asked her to be quiet. When the song ended I explained what I had found in the box. She listened attentively, and I noticed she was a little bit nervous. I asked her if she knew anything about it. "No idea," she answered. Then she changed the subject.

When we got back to her house I asked her again.

"You really don't know anything?"

"No," she answered firmly.

I held her by the wrist as she was about to get out of the car and I pulled her in. I kissed her neck and groped her breasts. She pulled away from me, grabbed my face with both her hands and studied me for a long time.

"What am I going to do with you?" she said.

"Love me," I answered without thinking.

"Do you really want me to love you?" she asked, surprised.

I leaned in to kiss her again. She put a finger on my chin and pushed me back.

"Ask Tania," she said.

"What are you talking about?"

She pointed at the radio.

"The song lyrics. Ask her."

She didn't say anything else. She got out of the car without saying good-bye and walked inside.

• • •

EXHAUSTED, I MADE my way home. I sadly summoned up the images of Margarita's and Rebecca's naked bodies, the texture of their skin, their flavor. It pained me to know I was losing them.

I drove slowly, watching people, sizing them up, like the nights when Gregorio and I combed the streets looking for someone to fight with. We did it for the sheer pleasure, the addiction to violence. We didn't gang up on anyone; on the contrary, we were drawn to the surprise, the risk, the possibility of running into someone fiercer than ourselves. That was how we ended up taking on four or five at a time, like tough guys, to prove that we could. And of course we could, even if they beat the shit out of us. Because it wasn't about winning, it was about feeling the fists, the busted flesh. One's own, another's.

Several nights we were taken down; like the time when we misjudged a trio of hefty men who turned out to be a union leader's bodyguards. They cracked our toughness with their boots and pistol butts. We ended up lying in the gutter with our lips split and noses crushed. We didn't give a shit. It was part of the fun.

One Friday, when I went to pick up Gregorio, I found him worried, tense, with no desire to leave the house. After much insistence, he agreed to go for a spin around the neighborhood. As a condition, he said we should take it easy.

After driving around for an hour, we stopped in front of a store to buy some Pepsis and sat on the hood of the car to drink them. Gregorio was apathetic, reduced to muttering monosyllables.

He began to bore me. I left him alone and went into the store to buy some doughnuts. As I was paying for them, I heard a dull thud behind me: Gregorio had rolled off the hood and was lying on the sidewalk, scratching his arms manically.

I quickly picked him up by the chest and put him in the car.

The store owner looked out his window and asked if we needed any help. I said we didn't. I drove away, flooring the accelerator.

I decided to take him to a nearby welfare clinic. Gregorio was squirming on the seat, moaning, "They're eating me, they're eating me." We entered the parking lot, and as I was heading for the emergency wing, Gregorio grabbed me by the forearm.

"Let's get out of here," he ordered, with an unbalanced look on his face.

"What's wrong with you? Fuck!" I demanded.

"Let's go." He repeated.

I made a U-turn and we left. I stopped a few blocks farther on.

"Are you okay?" I asked.

He nodded. His face was pale. His left ring finger was trembling slightly.

"What's the matter?" I asked.

He clumsily explained that the earwigs were multiplying by the thousands inside of him, and that they were starting to eat his innards; that at night he woke up and saw how fistfuls of earwigs were flowing out of his mouth and nose and wriggling between the sheets. The most minimal shift would make the earwigs invade him again, entering through his nails, his scalp, his anus. He also confessed that when he masturbated, instead of semen he ejaculated small brown balls: compacted insects that, as soon as they hit the floor, scattered, only to rush back at him.

"I can feel them chew at me," he said. "They're eating me alive right now, I swear, they're eating me alive."

I TOOK HIM HOME. He asked me to stay and look after him.

"I can't beat them alone," he said. "I can't."

I spent the night with him, without either of us able to sleep. In the middle of the night, he sat up in bed. He sat on the edge of the mattress and calmly stated that the only way he would ever be free of the earwigs was to lie down beside a human corpse, still warm.

This was ridiculous. Nevertheless, he insisted: "It's my only option."

We didn't speak of it again until the following week, as we were scouting the streets.

"We need to kill somebody," he said without emotion.

His theory was simple: He had to kill a man (a woman wouldn't work), split him open, and lie down next to him so that the smell of entrails, still fuming, would attract the mass of insects eating away at his insides.

"It's my only option," he repeated.

To prove that he was serious, he took out a switchblade and opened it.

"What? Are you going to kill me?" I joked.

"No." He answered drily.

"Why don't you stop fucking around and put that thing away?" I said.

He smiled sarcastically.

"Are you scared?"

I didn't pay attention to him and kept driving. It seemed like one of his many boasts, and wasn't worth getting upset over. Suddenly, as I slowed down to turn a corner, Gregorio pointed at a skinny kid, no more than fifteen years old, who walked distractedly down the sidewalk.

"That one," he shouted.

Gregorio jumped from the moving car and ran toward him. Taking him by surprise, he threw him against the wall. The boy tried to turn around, but Gregorio held the knife to his back.

"Hold still."

I stopped the car in the middle of the street and headed toward them. Gregorio was breathing agitatedly, beside himself.

"Take it easy," I said.

He looked at me spitefully. He grabbed the teen by his hair, held the blade to his throat, and forced him to kneel.

The kid started to beg pitifully for his life. Aggravated, Gregorio shook him to shut him up.

"Let him go," I begged.

Gregorio smirked.

"It's my only choice."

There was no one on the street other than the three of us. The teenager's screams could be heard loud and clear. Gregorio pressed the knife against his neck and when I thought he was about to make the definitive incision, he pulled the blade away.

"It's just a joke," he said, looking at me. "It's a fucking joke."

He started to laugh. He ordered the boy to get up and he obeyed.

Gregorio faced him, staring at him straight in the eyes.

"Get out of here," he said, and kissed him on the forehead.

The boy ran away into the dark side streets.

"It was a joke . . ." Gregorio repeated in a whisper.

ONE NIGHT, six months after that incident, Gregorio's parents found him sitting on a dining room chair gushing blood from his bare feet. He had cut them with the same knife. He thought that, due to the laws of gravity, the earwigs would flow out with the bloodstream and he would finally be rid of them.

Gregorio severed veins and tendons. The damage was such that he required several reconstructive procedures. He was unable to walk for two months. While still in recovery, he was moved to the psychiatric hospital, to the ward with the dangerous patients, the one with the "real crazies," as Gregorio called them.

"We're losing him," mumbled his father, worried, after I accompanied him to one of the very brief visits his son was allowed.

I'd seen him sedated, babbling idiocies, tied to the bed with his feet wrapped in bandages.

"We're losing him," he said again and rested his head on the steering wheel. He cried in a way he always hid from his children. "Don't cry," he'd order, "you look like a sissy." They'd grow quiet, swallowing their tears. Now he was sobbing disconsolate, without holding back, moaning, "We're losing him, we're losing him."

And we did: Gregorio slowly left us, disappearing by degrees into the inaccessible landscape of his madness.

THREE DAYS after his wounds healed, Gregorio cut two toes off his right foot and put them in his mouth. That same night I had sex with his sister on his living room carpet.

I GOT BACK HOME at two in the morning. Upon closing the garage door, I spotted a small kitten in the corner. It was wet and shivering. I moved closer to it and it hissed, frightened. I wanted to catch it to dry and feed it. Still, when I reached out my hand, he swiped and managed to scratch me. I pulled back and the cat crouched, ready to attack again. I clapped three times loudly so that it would get out of the garage. It jumped and darted under the car and hid inside the motor by climbing the front axle.

I decided to leave it alone and went in the house. The scratch had left a thin string of blood on the back of my hand. I washed and disinfected. It was a precaution I always used to take when hurt by animals after Roberto Donneaud, my cousin, almost had to have his right thumb amputated when a parrot bite led to a severe infection.

I found a note from my mother on the nightstand: "Tania called, said she wasn't going to stay at home tonight, that if you want to, you can call her at Laura Luna's house: 803–52–74."

803–52–74 was a nonexistent phone number, a code to inform me that she'd be waiting at room 803.

I hesitated to go. I anxiously wanted to be with her, to kiss her, to make love to her, to listen to her, and for her to listen to me. But I was also afraid of her. I was afraid of confronting her, of not knowing what to say, of provoking her, of remaining silent, fighting, humiliating ourselves—of losing her.

I was exhausted and had to take a cold shower in order to wake up. I quickly got dressed, wrote my father a note saying that I'd bring the car back in the evening, and left.

I pulled into the Motel Villalba, drove around the parking lot, made sure the curtains were drawn in 803 and stopped in front of the reception area. I shut off the motor, got out of the car, and activated the alarm. I looked around. Despite the fact that it was early morning, several rooms were occupied. The dark-skinned employee stealthily emerged from a hallway and surprised me as I was counting the empty rooms.

"Evening," he mumbled.

From his tone of voice, I could tell he hadn't recognized me.

"What's up?" I greeted.

He studied my face lit by the blue neon sign.

"What can I do for you?" he asked, servile and gruff.

I smiled. How could he be so bad at recognizing faces?

"You don't remember me?" I asked.

"No," he answered drily.

"I rent 803."

He looked at me doubtfully for a moment and after a few moments nodded.

"Oh, now I remember. You're the guy who wanted to buy the gun."

"That's the one."

"Sorry, it's just that I see so many clients, and all of them at night, that, well, it's hard to keep track."

"So, are you gonna sell me the piece?"

He scratched the base of his skull and shook his head.

"See, the thing is, I told one of the guys about your idea, and the idiot told the boss, and so the boss took the gun away so I wouldn't be tempted."

I didn't believe him, but we both said we were sorry not to have done it earlier. I asked him to take care of the car and requested the key to 803. He searched his pockets and handed me a key.

"It's the master key," he warned. "Don't lose it."

I took it and squeezed it in my hand.

"Don't worry about it," I told him.

He took out a flashlight and turned it on.

"I'm gonna get back to work," he muttered. He turned away and continued his rounds.

. . .

TANIA'S BLACK JETTA was parked in the garage, behind the drawn curtains. I put my hand on the hood. It was cold—she must have arrived at least two hours earlier. I walked into the room. Tania was sleeping, naked, barely covered by one of the sheets. She was lit by a streetlight filtering through the curtain. I looked at her for a while in silence and she seemed more beautiful than ever.

I got naked and lay down next to her. I hugged her from behind and she sleepily grabbed one of my fingers. I started to lick the back of her neck. Tania shuddered and her skin rose slightly. She turned and kissed my mouth. I lowered my hands, grabbed her hips and pulled her toward me. Our stomachs touched. Still groggy, she pushed herself up with her left leg and straddled my thighs. She opened her eyes, looked at my face, and stroked my forehead.

"I thought you weren't going to come," she whispered.

I kissed her on the lips.

"Sorry," I said.

She smiled and lay on my chest.

"No, I'm sorry."

We made love slowly, without talking. No fury, no gymnastics. Just the slow ripple of our bodies.

For the first time in several weeks, we had a simultaneous orgasm. It was a calm, basic orgasm, and when we finished we fell asleep with me still inside her.

. . .

JUST BEFORE DAWN, I noticed her kneeling on the mattress, watching me.

"What's the matter?" I asked.

"Nothing," she answered in a low voice.

"So?"

She smiled and shrugged her shoulders.

"I was just looking at you."

I sat up and held her.

"Go back to sleep," I said.

She lay back and rested her forehead on my chest. I noticed she was sobbing. I touched her chin and lifted it up.

"What's wrong?"

She brushed the hair away from her eyes. She mopped up her tears with her forearm.

"Do you love me?" she asked, wrinkling her brow as if she were making an effort not to cry again.

"Lots."

"Really?"

"Really."

She seemed to calm down. She slowly let her head drop and curled up on my lap, facing my inner thigh.

"What about you?" I asked.

She softly bit my thigh as an answer. I kissed her shoulder and with the tips of my fingers traced a path down her spine. Tania exhaled a moan and stretched.

"No, please," she mumbled.

I kept my trajectory and lowered my finger to the end of her coccyx.

"Don't go on," she asked.

I slid my fingers down even farther and started stroking circles around her anus.

"Manuel," she whispered and bit my thigh again. I wet her anus with some vaginal fluid and inserted my middle finger.

She contorted forward and backward to a rhythm that made my finger go deeper and deeper. Her snaking motion accelerated. When it seemed as if Tania was going to reach orgasm she suddenly stopped and gripped my finger with her anus.

"Are you going to marry me?" she asked.

"I don't know," I answered, "it's a long way away."

"Yes or no."

It took me a moment to answer. She loosened her muscles and shifted to one side. I moved my finger to avoid it slipping, but she turned her hips to push it out. She seemed more sad than upset.

"Yes!" I exclaimed out loud.

Tania looked at me skeptically.

"Yes," I repeated, "I will marry you."

She brought her hand to her face and started to laugh.

"Don't listen to me, I'm crazy," she said, and hid behind a pillow.

Her body convulsed with laughter. I took the pillow away and held her head in my hands.

"Stop fucking around."

She calmed down and sighed.

"I don't understand you," I said and threw the pillow onto the floor.

She picked it up and put it on her stomach.

"I'm all confused," she mumbled.

"Me too," I said.

"No, you're not," she said firmly.

"How do you know?"

"I just do," she murmured.

She closed her eyes, curled up under the covers, and asked me to hold her. She fell asleep as I caressed her shoulders.

The sun rose. I carefully pulled away from her and headed toward the window. The day was clear, no clouds, no rain. Tania snored slightly and I turned to look at her. She must have been dreaming; she was making little noises with her lips.

I sat next to her. I looked at her and imagined her in old age. I imagined, on her face, the blister of years: the sunken eyes, weak mouth, worn teeth, the hanging jaw. I imagined her stomach stretched from pregnancies, her dry thighs, her weak forearms, her lessened breasts.

If I married her, what would we talk about sixty years later? What would we remember? Would she sleep next to me this unselfconsciously? Would we make love, kissing our toothless mouths? Who would die first?

I lay down next to her, hugged her again, and slowly fell asleep.

I awoke at noon. It was hot and the sun was shining straight into the room. Tania wasn't in bed. I sat up and heard the shower running. I walked into the bathroom and sat on the toilet cover.

"Hey," said Tania, looking at me from behind the transparent shower curtain. She smiled and blew me a kiss.

I asked her to turn and face the wall. I wanted to pee and was embarrassed to do it in front of her. She did, without trying to peek.

"What do you want for breakfast?" I asked when I was done.

"The usual," she answered.

"The usual" consisted of a plate of tamales and a cup of chocolate atole. We used to buy them on Saturday and Sunday mornings from a woman who set up on the opposite corner from the motel.

"It's late," I said. "I'll check if she's still there."

Tania called me over. I approached her, she stuck her head out from behind the shower curtain and kissed me on the mouth.

"You don't know how much I love you."

I took a step back and looked at her. She covered her breasts with her arms.

"What are you looking at?" she asked, laughing.

"Nothing."

"Then stop peeking," she said and splashed my eyes.

I kissed her again and set out for breakfast.

THE MOTEL WAS EMPTY: Sunday was the day with the least movement. "Football Sunday is a day for chastity and family," Camariña used to say. I greeted Pancho, who was sweeping the driveway to 813.

"Hey, Pancho," I called out.

Pancho raised his chin, smiled when he recognized me, waved his hand and kept sweeping.

I ran into Camariña. He had placed a table and chair in the middle of the corridor and was watching the Atlante versus Celaya match on a portable TV.

"Hey, what's up?" he asked cordially.

"Nothing new."

He leaned toward me and whispered:

"You made up with your girlfriend, huh?"

I assented. In a paternal gesture, Camariña squeezed my forearm.

"I'm glad," he said.

On the TV the sportscaster raised his voice over a dangerous play near the goal and Camariña turned to look at the screen.

"I'll see you in a bit," I said and went on.

The sun was shining and the air was transparent and cold. As I tried to cross the street I sidestepped a taxi. I was happy, in a good mood.

I found the woman clearing up. I barely made it in time to buy two red tamales and two green ones. There were no sweet ones, Tania's favorite, and no chocolate atole.

The woman wrapped the tamales in a sheet of newspaper and handed them over to me. I burned my hand on the still boiling water that dripped down the corn leaves and dropped the tamales. The woman laughed, picked them up, and put them in a plastic bag.

"Here you are," she said, with a trace of jest.

I went back to the motel. As I crossed the street, Camariña gestured for me to come over.

"Come with me," he said.

He turned off the TV and we went into his office. He asked me to sit down. He took out a cigar, lit it with his metal lighter, and sat behind his desk. He settled in, then brought his face closer to mine, like someone who wants to talk business.

"I heard you wanted to buy the gun from Pánfilo," he said, right off the bat.

His tone of voice was neutral, without any inflection to indicate if he was angry about this or not.

"Yes," I confirmed.

"And why do you want a gun?"

I didn't know how to answer him. Camariña gave the cigar a long drag and exhaled the smoke to one side. The wisps rose, hovered against the roof, and disappeared out one of the ventilation shafts.

"It ain't good that a kid like you should carry a gun," he condemned.

I shrugged my shoulders.

"You never know," I said.

Camariña opened a drawer and took out the gun. He put it on a red cloth and lined up six golden bullets.

"It's pretty, isn't it?"

"Yeah."

"I bought that gun many years ago from a crooked salesman at La Merced market. I've only fired it twice, to try it out."

Camariña held it up to the light and looked at it proudly.

"I thought I was going to get held up every payday and see: no need."

He cleaned a fingerprint off the barrel with the red cloth.

"I just sent it to the gunsmith; he left it as good as new. Look at it shine, look how smoothly the cylinder turns."

He touched it for a while, then put it back on the red cloth and pushed it over toward me.

"Here, it's yours," he said.

"Why?"

"Because I say so."

"But . . ."

"Nothing, man, it's yours; take it as a payment for the jacket."

"I gave you the jacket," I protested.

"Then I'm giving you the gun."

I ended up accepting it, and to thank him, I gave Camariña a green tamale.

I FOUND TANIA sitting on the bench in front of the dressing table. She was combing her hair, naked (in accordance to an agreement we made where, while we were in 803, neither of us was allowed wear clothes, unless it was too cold).

"Did you get the tamales?"

"Yes," I answered and put the bag down on the dresser.

"Were there any sweet ones?"

"No," I said and put the gun and bullets in front of her, "but look what I got."

Tania turned to look at me, wide-eyed and perturbed.

"Camariña gave it to me," I clarified.

She grew pale and swept the bullets away with the side of her hand.

"Get it away from me."

"It's okay," I said.

"Get it away," she ordered.

I picked up the gun, cocked it, and aimed at my reflection in the mirror.

"What are you doing?"

I pulled the trigger and the pistol went "click." Tania jumped and covered her face with her hands.

"You're an idiot," she muttered.

She wrapped herself in a towel and locked herself in the bathroom. I decided to put the gun away in the car. When I got back, Tania was getting dressed.

"I was just playing," I told her.

"Well, your little games are fucking stupid," she retorted.

She put on her sweater, grabbed her purse, and headed to the door. I grabbed her wrists.

"Don't leave," I implored.

She tried to break free.

"Leave me alone."

"No, not till you calm down."

We struggled for a while until she raised her hands.

"All right, I won't leave, but let me go."

"You promise?"

"Let go," she ordered, in a low voice.

I released her wrists and she sat on the bed.

"You scare me, Manuel, you scare me . . ."

I sat next to her and hugged her.

"I swear, I was just joking."

"No, you weren't," she said, raising her voice, "you wanted to scare me."

She tried to stand up and I pushed her back onto the bed.

"I swear I didn't."

I started to kiss her as I repeated, "I swear, I swear." She stopped resisting, I undressed her and we made love again.

WE HAD TAMALES for breakfast, lying on the bed. Tania mentioned the possibility of getting a TV for the room. She suggested we buy one at Sears where we could pay it off in installments.

"We don't need one," I told her and turned one of her nipples as if it were a knob from an old TV. "We just have to turn this dial to whatever channel we like."

Tania laughed and pushed me.

"Don't be stupid," she said and rubbed her nipple.

I picked up the Ruvalcaba book that was lying on the nightstand and I asked why she had underlined the passage about the bureaucrats buying bread.

"Because."

"Do you know any bread-buying bureaucrats?" I asked mockingly.

"I used to," she mumbled and remained pensive.

Her languid expression made me jealous.

"An uncle of mine, my mother's brother," she went on, "used

to work in one of the commercial areas in the Department of Wildlife. One afternoon, after leaving the office, he went into a bakery to buy bread, and as he was paying, some robbers walked in."

She stopped for a moment and wet her lips.

"Because he refused to hand over the change, about five pesos, they shot him in the head . . ."

Suddenly she turned to me.

"I'd never told you?"

"No."

"He just lay there next to his bread bag. My aunt was left a widow with a two-year-old son and a ten-month-old baby . . ."

"How long ago was this?"

"I was little—it would've been around third or fourth grade of primary school. That was the first funeral I ever went to."

She choked up and hugged me, worried.

"Don't do anything crazy."

"What are you talking about?"

"I don't want you to die."

"I'm not going to die," I assured her. "I promise."

"I'm not going to die." Gregorio had uttered just these words one May afternoon. He'd just been released from the hospital with two amputated toes. "I'm not going to die," he reaffirmed. Tania hugged him guiltily. A few days earlier, after making love to me, she'd whispered, "I hope he dies." She wanted Gregorio to vanish into thin air, just like that. She wanted him to stop hurting her. She couldn't deal with the fact that he'd gone crazy. She couldn't tolerate loving both him and me. She simply couldn't bear him and had wanted him to die.

"I'm not going to die," I repeated.

Tania kissed me warily.

"Give the gun back."

"No!"

"Please."

"No."

She squeezed me tightly.

"Don't do anything stupid."

"Never," I said, "never . . ."

WE DECIDED TO LEAVE at five PM. As we were getting dressed, I told Tania about the box Gregorio had left. She listened intently, focused on my descriptions of the photographs and packets. She said she didn't know Jacinto Anaya. She didn't know about the song lyrics either.

"Margarita told me you might know."

Tania reddened.

"And how the fuck does that bitch know what I think?" she exclaimed, irritated.

I found her anger excessive.

"Don't talk about her like that, she's your friend."

"My friend?" she asked. "Don't you mean your friend?"

"Both of ours."

Tania shook her head and said nothing else. As we finished dressing I went over to kiss her. She kissed me coldly.

"What's the matter?"

"Nothing," she answered drily, and we left the room and I opened the garage curtains. Tania got into her car and lowered her window.

"Bye," I said.

"Bye."

She gave me a tight-lipped peck on the cheek, started the car, and drove off. I went back into the room and sat on the bed. The empty room weighed on me, as if the air without Tania were thicker. Maybe she was right: We needed to buy a TV.

WHEN I WAS ABOUT to get into the car, Pancho called out to me.

"It's dripping something," he pointed out.

I ducked to see what was leaking. It didn't look like oil, water, or gasoline. I reached under and touched the front axle. It was blood.

I asked Pancho for a piece of cardboard so I could check under the car. I found a mess of hair, meat, and bones. The cat that hid in the motor had been torn apart, probably by the radiator fan. I poked at the remains with a clothes hanger and removed the animal in strips. It stank of urine and decomposition. Pancho found this very funny and he'd laugh every time I pulled out a foot or part of its back. "It looks like you're giving your car an abortion," he said with a humor that made me sad.

I ARRIVED BACK HOME at dusk. I tucked the gun under my shirt so my parents wouldn't see it. I quickly ran upstairs and hid the gun in a drawer in my bathroom. My precautions were unnecessary: There was no one home.

An hour later, Luis returned from Cuernavaca. He was accompanied by a girl I didn't know. He introduced her as his girlfriend. I can't remember her name, much less her face. She was entirely insipid. (Two weeks later, my brother broke up with her.)

A couple of hours later, my parents arrived. My father looked as if he didn't feel very well. He was pale and out of sorts. My mother explained that they'd gone to eat tacos and that they hadn't agreed with him. I heard him vomit several times, without complaining. He tried to be discreet when sick, as opposed to my mother, for whom the slightest ailment was the perfect excuse for drama.

I had dinner with Luis and the girlfriend, who looked worried every time we heard my father's loud retching. "You're daddy's really sick," she said in a saccharine tone between mouthfuls. She didn't seem to care that the bouquet of gastric juices permeated the house.

I WENT TO BED EARLY. At midnight, my father woke me up by touching me softly on the shoulder. Startled, I opened my eyes, and then relaxed once I made out his features in the dark.

"Where did you sleep yesterday?" he asked.

I didn't answer.

"How do you feel?" I asked.

"So so."

He sat down next to me. His face was lit by the light of the moon, streaming through the curtains.

"And you, how are you?" he asked.

"Fine."

"Really?"

"Yes," I answered without conviction.

He proposed that the four of us go on a family vacation. Like when we were kids.

"Let's go to Puerto Vallarta," he said.

I smiled at the suggestion. We used to go to Puerto Vallarta to celebrate Christmas and New Year's. I grew up with the idea that Christmas meant heat, beach, and scrawny, yellow palm trees decked out in colored lightbulbs. The snowmen, the white landscapes on the greeting cards, and the fake pine trees felt contradictory. They simply didn't make sense.

My dad got up, but before he left the room he repeated, "Let's go to Puerto Vallarta." He closed the door and I lay there remembering the old, sweaty Christmas dinners under the ceiling fans, raising glasses of warm cider, eating recently defrosted turkey.

THE NEXT DAY I dressed in a black, long-sleeve shirt to go to school: I'd had enough days where I was reminded of my scars. It would be difficult to justify my absences to my professors, who prided themselves on being rigorous and demanding. Someone dying was not a good enough excuse for failing to hand in a project or model. ("What the hell does your aunt Francisca have to do with that mess?" a teacher once barked at a student. He'd handed in a smudged project, sketched on his lap during the funeral mass for his favorite aunt, who had been run over by a soda delivery truck with no brakes.) Professor Molina, the head of department, claimed that designing houses was one of the most serious responsibilities in the world. He used to say: "You grow up, sleep, fight, love, fornicate, eat, hate, and die in a house. These aren't just constructions, boys, they're life's sacred spaces." He was right, but I wasn't willing to listen to sermons that morning. No matter how hard you try, life's sacred spaces can't compete with life itself, and not even two hundred perfectly constructed walls can silence the sound of a gunshot midafternoon.

Luckily, none of the professors held my absence against me.

. . .

IN THE FIRST CLASS I ran into Rebecca. She greeted me, distant and nervous. She sat toward the front of the class instead of all the way at the back, next to me, like we used to. While the teacher lectured on the resistance of concrete, I never took my eyes off the point where her neck and back connected. Once I heard that if you stare fixedly at that point, you can force the person to turn around and look at you. Rebecca never turned around, not then, not on any other occasion, and the exercise only succeeded in making me want to kiss her neck intensely.

I found the classes to be generally bland and pointless, except for Modern Literature, the only optional course I was taking that semester. I'd registered for two reasons: because the professor seemed disdainful of conventional teaching methods, and because he was obsessed with the Beat generation. Kerouac, Burroughs, Ginsberg—they were the only writers he'd talk about. The others—Faulkner, Rulfo, Joyce, Martín Luís Guzmán—he'd barely mention. Personally, I couldn't care less about the Beats, and the fact that I gave literature a shot was only because Gregorio considered *On the Road* to be the coolest book he'd ever read ("It's like an album by the Doors," he used to say).

I was more interested in the Beats' life than their work, especially Burroughs, who Gregorio detested. "He's an old faggot," he said when he found out that Burroughs was openly gay (Gregorio was so homophobic that he was capable of viciously beating someone only on suspicion). He was into Kerouac: ex-Marine, handsome, ex-football player. "Now *he* was a tough motherfucker," he claimed. In the end, however, he wasn't, and it was Burroughs, sexual preference and all, who outlived them, including Kerouac and Gregorio.

That morning, the professor told us how Burroughs had killed his wife in a gloomy Mexico City apartment when, totally drunk, he blew her forehead open playing William Tell.

At the end of the class I approached the teacher. Trying to stick with the Burroughs theme, I explained that I'd missed class the previous week because my best friend had blown his head off playing a solitary William Tell.

"You mean he killed himself?"

I nodded. The teacher smiled and patted me on the back indulgently.

"Excellent excuse, Manuel, very literary," he said. Idiot. "I'll ignore your absences because you're original, but make sure you catch up on the work you missed."

He winked and left the room without letting me say another word. I saw him walk down the corridor. I walked the other way toward the faculty parking lot, found his car, and punctured his four tires with my Swiss Army knife. I waited for them to deflate and left.

I went back home, furious, convinced that I should drop out of college, abandon architecture, and leave this small world of stern and mediocre professors. I decided to go relax at a nearby pool, where for thirty pesos you could stay indefinitely.

Luckily, the pool was empty, and I was able to swim as many laps as I liked, without having to swerve around children in floaties or old women doing aqua-aerobics. When I was almost done, a bland, pudgy blonde appeared, dressed in a garish sapphire swimsuit with yellow stripes. She seemed familiar. She got into the water without looking at me and started to flail her arms around in an awkward, cumbersome way that at times looked something like a breast stroke. After awhile, I managed to place her. She was a famous soap-opera star. "The queen of sensuality" according to cheap tabloids. I took a good look at her and even went underwater with my goggles to stare at her legs. They had cellulite. Pounds of it. Her breasts looked a little more appetizing, but also probably had cellulite ("Tits like sponge cake," Gregorio called them, "greasy and full of holes").

When I got out of the pool, I noticed that two bodyguards were intently watching over the woman with the flat sensuality. All in vain, since there was no one left to want her.

I arrived home a little calmer and found my mother. She greeted me with a hug and several kisses. I found it strange that she should be so affectionate. She then recited the messages that had been left for me: at two-fourteen Tania had called, Joaquín at five after three, and a friend from college had called at three twenty-two to remind me about a group project we had to do (we had to design some Barragán-style crap, with water mirrors and thick walls).

My mother offered to make some chicken sandwiches. Her effort to be caring and attentive was apparent. She and I never really understood each other; we were alike in the things we should have differed in, and differed in those we should have shared.

My mother was unable to keep up her jovial mood for very long. She accompanied me while I ate, we spoke trivially about trivia, and then, a little sick of each other, we retired to our own things.

Before I went upstairs, she called out to me.

"I forgot to give you this," she said, and handed me a letter. "It arrived this morning in the mail."

I thanked her and kept on my way.

• • •

THE LETTER HAD no return address. The writing on the envelope was familiar, but I couldn't immediately identify it.

I opened it. Inside there was a wrinkled, yellowish paper with a single phrase written on it: "Now the night buffalo will dream of you."

Nothing else. At first I laughed out loud, thinking it was a stupid joke. Then I sat down on the mattress, rattled. Gregorio had written that, there was no doubt about it. His long, angry script stood out.

I got up without knowing exactly what to do. The blow had been dealt with precision. From his urn and his ashes, Gregorio was stalking me again. I wouldn't be able to confront him, not even insult him. I also couldn't tear up the letter and forget it: the threats and secret messages would probably keep coming, one after the other.

I tried to calm down. Gregorio couldn't beat me, much less with some moronic phrase. I went out into the hallway. My mother was downstairs, in the kitchen. I went to her room and rummaged through her medicine cabinet. I found some sleeping pills and took triple the recommended dosage. I went back to my room and lay down, waiting for the pills to start working. Foggy, I grabbed the letter. The writing on the envelope was different from Gregorio's. The postage date was February the twenty-fourth, two days after Gregorio's suicide. Somebody was following the plan.

The key was in the handwriting. Almost asleep, I tried to look over the types of handwriting that I knew: Margarita, Tania, Rebecca, Joaquín, my father, my mother, Luis, Margarita, Rebecca . . .

• • •

I GOT UP AT MIDNIGHT, afraid. Again, I had felt a stifling, humid breath on the back of my neck. I tried to run away, to jump out of bed, but I was unable to move. The sleeping pills had me in a state of semi-consciousness. I noticed lights, noise, voices. My legs, my arms didn't respond.

After about an hour, I managed to turn on the light. My head was throbbing and my tongue felt swollen. I walked into the bathroom and gargled some water. I looked at my face in the mirror: It still looked like a stranger's.

Under the door, I found a note from my mother with phone messages. At 5:08 PM, my friend from college had called, annoyed, because I hadn't shown up to work on the project with the group. At 6:02 PM, Tania called, and at 6:25 PM, Doctor Macías's secretary called to ask why I hadn't gone to my appointment. I had completely forgotten and was happy to have stood him up.

The handwriting on the envelope started to worry me. Why the fuck had anyone volunteered for Gregorio's sick machinations? I thought it might be Doctor Macías himself, and I found the idea amusing: the prestigious psychiatrist, slave to his most tormented patient. I imagined both of them making a blood pact and Macías swearing eternal loyalty. He probably also had a buffalo tattooed on his left biceps.

This helped distract me a bit. I put my pajamas on and got back into bed. I was about to turn off the light when I suddenly remembered where I had seen the script on the envelope. I went to the closet and took out Gregorio's box. I looked through the pieces of paper in the package with the black ribbon. I grabbed one of them and compared the traces. Yes: Jacinto Anaya had written the song lyrics as well as the address on the envelope.

I tried to contact Macías. Maybe he knew about Gregorio's plan and had been trying to warn me. I called his office. No one answered. I called his beeper and sent him a message to get in touch with me. He didn't.

I called Tania's house. She had probably received a similar letter. Her sister answered sleepily. I asked her to put Tania on the phone. She said that it was no time to be calling in the first place and hung up. They didn't get along. She was jealous of Tania. She said that Tania was given too many privileges, that her parents let her do whatever she wanted, while she, because she was older, was always kept in check. She was wrong. They were both headstrong and capricious, only Tania was more decisive.

I tried calling Margarita, but her father answered and I hung up. I came to think that she was also involved in Gregorio's game. Then I hesitated; she was probably another victim.

I resolved to be patient and not pay attention to Gregorio's cheap confabulations. I threw the box into a corner and turned on the TV.

I SPENT THE NIGHT with insomnia, staring at newscasts. I jolted at dawn, certain that an earwig had come out of my mouth. I lifted the sheets and found nothing.

I left the room. The doors to the other rooms were closed. I imagined my parents sleeping in their bedroom, next to each other, dreaming their respective dreams, keeping their own worlds intact. I imagined my father getting up in the half-dark, drinking water from the glass on the nightstand, rubbing his eyes, so close and still so far away from my sleeping mother. I imagined her dreaming about all the different job opportunities she'd lost and which she considered fundamental to her life. I imagined my brother dreaming of his insipid girlfriends, his friends, his trips, his preoccupations, and his bland desires.

I went downstairs into the living room and headed over to the wooden bar my father had built. He had built it so it would be "his" place, where he could get together with his friends to chat and drink rum and Cokes, and they'd sit on the benches while he served them from the other side of the bar. Only twice in thirteen years did I see him get together like that with his friends. The other times he was alone, in the early morning, drinking rum and Coke with lime and ice (served like only he knew how), solving crossword puzzles from the pages of the *Excelsior.*

I never drank, not a drop. I had never known what it was like to be drunk. Neither had Gregorio. Drinking seemed like something faggots did. Nevertheless, that morning, I craved drinking my father's treasured Cuban rum down to the last drop. Maybe that way the earwigs, the breathing on my neck, life itself, would have some meaning. But no, drinking was for sissies.

I sat on one of the benches and opened a bag of Japanese peanuts that my father always kept at hand, part of his obsession to be a good host. I chewed, crushing them between my molars. That noise always bothered my brother. He thought I was doing it to annoy him. The truth is, I liked to hear them crunch.

I could hear the water running in my parents' bathroom. My dad was probably having a shower, getting ready for another day of work as a bank manager. He wasn't always like this, even though I can't visualize him without his banker's suit and wine-colored briefcase (an image that filled me with pride as a boy: the image of a confident, important man).

I remembered when he confessed he'd smoked marijuana, some ten, twelve times, hidden in the college bathrooms, at parties, inside a beat-up Volkswagen. He showed me a photograph from back then. He and his friends were in it, with their hair falling over their eyebrows, thick sideburns, flowery shirts and ridiculous bell-bottoms. The same friends who, twenty-five, thirty years later, would no longer share his bar, his conversation, his heavenly rum and Cokes prepared with lime and ice.

My father finished showering. I imagined him quietly getting dressed so as not to disturb my mother, knotting his tie, splashing his face with expensive, outdated aftershave. Then I saw him descending the staircase. His expression was different from most days, more relaxed, free of the usual gestures of a father or a husband. He looked like a man getting ready to go to work. Just a man. Plain, simple, maybe a little clumsy. A man.

He left, closing the door carefully so as not to make any noise. I imagined all the times he left early in the morning for a business meeting when he could've gone to meet a beautiful woman at a motel. All those times he missed smoking pot, fighting in bars, eating tacos and running away without paying, watching midnight porn. All the times he was tempted to leave us, to get in the car next to the beautiful woman and drive down a straight and endless highway. All the times he could have and didn't.

Maybe this was the right time to run, so that twenty, thirty years later, one of my sons didn't see me walking quietly down the stairs so as not to wake the rest of the family.

I didn't run and went back to my room.

• • •

THE REST OF THE MORNING I remained locked in my room, distraught. It was clear that Gregorio wanted me to know that Jacinto Anaya was his scribe and accomplice. He'd left enough clues. But for what? For me to seek him out and confront him? Or would finding him lead to the next part of the plan? I couldn't ignore the trap. I couldn't avoid it either. I had to keep going.

Impulsively, I grabbed the box and opened the packet with the blue ribbon—the one whose content I was most afraid of. I had barely untied the knot when I encountered a photograph that was a message in itself. In it were Tania, Gregorio, and myself. It was taken the last day of high school. Each one of us had a copy signed by the other two. In this copy, my face and Tania's had been run through with a cigarette.

Then came a recent portrait of Tania. She was wearing a white blouse I'd given her at Christmas, and a silver necklace Gregorio had given her for their first anniversary. Then I found several newspaper cutouts from the movie section of *El Universal*. Some of the advertised movies were marked in blue ink with the showtimes underlined in red. There were also some pictures of Gregorio in the garden of the psychiatric ward. He was wearing blue jeans and a black T-shirt. You could see the buffalo tattooed on his left biceps. He was smiling and in one photograph blowing kisses at the photographer.

Next I found a box of matches with the name and address of a motel printed on it. It was a motel near the Villalba, probably the same one in which the lieutenant killed his lover. On the back of the matchbox, Gregorio had written a date, January fifth, and a phrase: "today, very close to the fire." The date coincided with one of the underlined showtimes for a movie in the newspaper cuttings.

I also found a poem from a book by Agustín García Delgado

that Tania liked very much and frequently quoted. It was transcribed on a typewriter. The poem was called "Room."

ROOM

Better to stay,
Outside a deathless burial awaits us,
Outside is a cemetery where a scarecrow
Armed in vigil
Frightens the blue crows of silence away.

In the vast early morning of the soul,
The pitiless rooster will not stop.
The sun that would silence him will never rise.
Never will our hands touch
The luminous edge of day.

Tania had dated the poem January eighth. In the margin, Gregorio had written: "today, inside the fire, deep inside."

After looking through a bunch of papers with cryptic messages on them, I found the key to understanding everything else. On the back of a receipt from a gas station near the psychiatric hospital, Tania had scrawled:

"My love, they won't let me in to see you. I'm desperate. This is the third time. I don't know what to do. The watchman who used to let me in is gone. But I'm here, waiting for you. Always, don't forget. I hope this note reaches you."

Below Tania had written two of the song lyrics that Jacinto Anaya had copied:

"Near you everything is new / it's being in the fire's center."

The receipt was from just six months ago. They'd both kept their relationship hidden from me. I hadn't expected this. I hadn't been capable of figuring out what was going on around me, and that was the most painful thing of all.

Gregorio's plan was working too well. Only the rage of a dead man could be so effective. I looked at the box and the mess of papers impregnated with vengeance. I piled them into a corner of the shower and set them on fire. The photographs started to curl and so did the newspaper cuttings, the hidden messages, the unopened packets.

Once the fire went out, I turned on the water so that it would wash the ashes into the drain. The room was left full of a cloud of smoke that made me cough. I sat on the floor, exhausted, short of breath, as if the fire had consumed all the oxygen in the room. I remained motionless for a few minutes, my eyes fixed on the drain as the ashes disappeared.

I felt incredibly tired.

I HAD NO CHOICE but to forget. Only by erasing the past could I face the pain. Now, more than ever, I had to love and trust Tania. I wouldn't reproach her at all.

No matter how much it hurt, I had to deal with the blow, I had to humbly assume that she possessed mysteries to which I had no access, in the same way that she had no access to mine.

I had to forget. Or at least try. Forgive. Forget.

Forget.

IT WASN'T POSSIBLE. In the evening I received another letter from Gregorio. Like the last one, the envelope bore Jacinto's handwriting. I tried to get rid of it, to burn it before I opened it. My curiosity won.

The letter had two pages. On the first, Gregorio warned: "You won't be able to run from the night buffalo."

The second page was a note that apparently Tania had sent to Gregorio at the hospital on January fifteenth of that year: "As soon as you get out of there, we'll go as far away as we can. I promise, my love. This time I mean it."

January fifteenth was the last time Gregorio checked into a psychiatric hospital. He left two weeks later, when Macías and his team decreed that he was ready to readapt. Twenty-two days later, he killed himself.

I dropped the letter. And no, there was no way out. Gregorio wouldn't let me forget. He'd rub the past and his secrets with Tania in my face until he beat me, if he hadn't beaten me already.

Tania had insisted, over and over, that her breakup with Gregorio was definitive, and that it was me she loved. Why, then, that late need to run away with him?

I put on the first thing that appeared in the closet: a pair of jeans and a navy blue T-shirt. I grabbed a jacket and headed out toward Macías's office. I needed to find Jacinto Anaya. I could think of no other way to stop Gregorio's attacks, at least momentarily.

I LEFT THE BEDROOM. My mother was watching TV in her room. Without telling her, I took her car keys. As I was pulling out of the garage, she looked out the window. She watched me impassively. I waved good-bye. Expressionless, she closed the curtain.

• • •

THE CARS WERE MOVING slowly down the avenue. A broken water main was flooding the central lanes, complicating the traffic flow. A Volkswagen tried to avoid the gridlock by climbing up onto the divider. As he did, he lightly hit my car. Instead of stopping, he tried to escape, but I caught up to him several blocks ahead. I cut him off. I got out, bent on beating the shit out of him. When he saw me coming he locked the doors. That he should stay inside pissed me off even more. I knocked on his window and shouted at him that he should pay for the damages. He looked at me timorously and slid over to the passenger seat. I picked up a large rock and smashed his windshield to pieces. Not even that would get him out of his car. With the same rock, I tried to shatter the window. Suddenly I realized that I was surrounded by dozens of curious onlookers. None of them seemed willing to intervene. They were just watching, expectant.

I stopped my attack and looked at my adversary. He was in his forties and looked like he worked in an office. He was terrified. I was disgusted by his frightened little eyes behind his glasses. Without dropping the rock, I crossed the ring of bystanders, got into my car, and drove off.

I DROVE DISTRAUGHT the rest of the way, with the rock in my right hand the whole time, even when I changed gears. It was once I'd reached Doctor Macías's office that I realized I still had it with me. I opened the window and, furious, threw it into an empty lot.

I sat in the car, listening to the radio to calm down. Macías shouldn't see me agitated. No, he shouldn't.

When I got out of the car, I looked at the clock on the tape deck: six-seventeen—the same hour Gregorio had killed himself. I walked into the office. In the waiting room was a tall, disheveled woman—God knows how old—with dyed hair. She was reading a magazine and paid no attention to me.

I walked up to the receptionist. She raised her eyes and asked me what she could do for me.

"I'm here to see Doctor Macías."

"Do you have an appointment?"

"Yes," I answered decisively.

"I don't remember having written it down," she said.

"I made the appointment with the doctor personally," I affirmed.

She asked me to repeat my name. She pulled out an agenda, opened it, and shook her head.

"The doctor's booked through the evening. I don't think he can see you."

"But . . ."

The receptionist interrupted me rudely.

"If you want, I can pencil you in for an appointment on the Wednesday after next. Is five o'clock okay?"

I leaned in and faced her.

"No, ma'am, it's not okay."

"It's just that the doctor . . ."

I ran my right index finger over her hand and I stroked her wrist. The woman was startled.

"Tell Macías I'm waiting for him, that I only came because he asked me to."

The receptionist moistened her lips and pretended to look calm.

"As soon as the six-fifty patient walks out, I'll tell him. You know he doesn't like to be interrupted. Is that okay?"

"That's okay."

Doctor Macías tended to his patients in fifty-minute intervals and left ten minutes between appointments. I looked at the wall clock: six twenty-seven. I sat down next to the woman with the reddish hair. The skin on her long hands was taut. Her face looked worn, with wrinkles in the edges of her lips that became more pronounced every time she took a drag off a menthol cigarette. She was probably younger than she looked.

I had no interest in any of the available magazines, so, to kill time, I imagined her naked, having sex. Her wrinkles probably weren't from her smoking habit, but from giving her husband a blow job, night after night, if she even had one. She was thin, but with a slightly bulky stomach. It was probably hairless, with some moles and stretchmarks from some pregnancy. Her legs didn't look firm. Her breasts did. They stuck out at a ninety-degree angle, pointy, apart from each other. She hunched as she read, although her neck had some poise, even though it wasn't a neck you'd want to kiss.

I peeked at the article she was reading. It was about a place near Australia where the wind blows so hard that the rain never hits the ground, ever. The woman became uncomfortable, shifted positions, and I couldn't read any more. I had no choice but to go back to imagining her naked.

I was entertained enough for time to go by quickly. At six-fifty on the dot, a fat guy a little younger than myself walked out of the office. Smiling, he signed a check and gave it to the receptionist. He looked stupidly happy. He let out a sonorous "have a good day" and left. The thin woman stood up and smoothed out her dress. "Just a moment," said the receptionist, and she walked into the office. A minute later she walked out, signaled to the woman to wait a little longer, and let me in.

• • •

MACÍAS WAS WAITING for me, sitting behind a desk, looking over some notes. Without looking at me, he signaled for me to sit down. I stayed standing. Macías finished up and got straight to it.

"We said we'd meet yesterday at six, right?"

"I think so," I answered.

"So?"

"I had other things to do."

"And so now you think you can come in here and disrespectfully harass my secretary and oblige my other patient to wait?"

"Obligate," I whispered.

Macías loved to use fancy words, even if he didn't know what they meant. He used them because they seemed tough.

"What did you say?"

"Nothing."

He clicked his tongue several times in disapproval.

"If you want, I'll leave," I proposed.

He looked at his watch and calculated.

"No, wait, I've got five minutes left and what I have to tell you won't take any longer."

He asked me to sit down. He pulled out an envelope from a drawer, walked around the desk, and sat in a chair next to me.

"You know what this is about, right?" he said, and threw the envelope onto the table.

I took it and opened it. Inside were three dead earwigs and a note: "Do you know what dead mice smell like?"

It wasn't hard to tell that Gregorio had written it. His aggressive penmanship stood out. The envelope was blank.

"This arrived on Friday night," Macías said. "Someone put it in my mailbox at home."

I put the envelope and the note on the desk and deliberately took my jacket off. Macías immediately turned to look at my scars.

"I don't know what it is," I told him.

"Are we going to play games, Manuel?" he asked petulantly.

"Which kind?"

Macías got up and looked at me sternly.

"You have serious problems, do you know that?"

I nodded.

"We all do," I added.

"No, young man, not all of us . . . you do, and I don't care if you want to work them out or not, but I'm going to ask you again, as a favor, and I repeat, *as a favor,* don't mess with me again, understand?"

"I didn't . . ."

Macías leaned both hands on the back of the chair and faced me.

"Don't play stupid. You were the only one who mentioned earwigs. No one else . . ."

It was pointless to argue with him. There was no need to mention the name Jacinto Anaya, or to tell him about all the letters I'd received myself.

"All right," I said, "is that it?"

"Yes."

He went back to sit on the armchair behind his desk.

"Could you tell Luisa, my secretary, to let my next patient in?"

"Yes."

Macías looked back at the notebook without making any attempt to say good-bye. His attitude bothered me.

"Doctor," I said.

"What?"

"Do you know what dead mice smell like?"

Macías lowered his head and looked at me over his glasses.

"Are you starting again?"

"No."

He brought his hand to his chin and clenched his jaw.

"Madness can be even more terrifying than death," he said slowly.

"I know."

"No, you don't."

"It's like rain that stops before it hits the ground, right?"

"No," he answered angrily, "now get the hell out."

I took my jacket and left. There was no need to inform the next patient. She was waiting anxiously behind the door. We exchanged glances. Her watery eyes gave me the impression that she was a woman who had resigned herself to imminent defeat, a defeat there was no way Macías could prevent. I let her through and closed the door behind her.

I walked toward the receptionist.

"What do you want?" she asked, hostile.

"Doctor Macías told me to ask you for the files on one of your patients: Jacinto Anaya."

"Patient files are confidential."

"The doctor authorized it."

"It's just that . . ."

"Do you want us to interrupt him?" I asked and pointed at the office.

The woman looked at me hesitantly. She typed on the computer and turned the monitor away so I wouldn't be able to see it. She wrote down his number on a card and gave it to me.

"What's his address?"

"That I can't give you," she explained, "and if you insist, then I am going to have to interrupt the doctor."

The phone number was enough.

"Thanks," I said, smiled kindly, and left.

. . .

"DO YOU KNOW what dead mice smell like?" The phrase came from a game, a pretty lame one, that Gregorio and I made up during high school:

"Do you know what it smells like between a woman's legs?" we'd say.

"Yes."

"Is it true that it smells like fish?"

"No!"

"So?"

"A mouse."

"A live mouse?"

"No, a dead one."

"And what do dead mice smell like?"

"What is smells like between a woman's legs."

The game started when Irma, a classmate everybody called "Chiquis," wore a very short dress to school and when she crossed her legs she briefly revealed a glimpse of her Mickey Mouse panties.

Eventually, the joke became code. "Do you know what dead mice smell like?" meant last night I fucked a woman. It was a way of alluding to sexual encounters.

I doubt Macías knew the code. It was too private, too much our own. I couldn't understand why Gregorio had sent it to him, but it set off uncontrollable pangs of jealousy. I deduced that, in one of his insane, exact triangulations, Gregorio was letting me know through Macías's letter that he'd finally penetrated Tania, spilled his semen inside her, and that the three earwigs symbolized precisely that semen.

Do you know what dead mice smell like? The more time went by the more incensed I became. I wanted to believe that

Gregorio was making fun of his psychiatrist, that he'd probably slept with his daughter, or wife, or lover. But what was the point in telling him with subtleties? No, Macías didn't deserve a letter like that; it would be foolish excess.

The mere idea that Gregorio could reach me through other people made me squirm. Soon he could corner me, edge me toward the abyss again. Despite his idiocy, Macías wasn't wrong: Madness, it's true, can be more terrifying than death.

FURIOUS, I HEADED toward Tania's house, ready to fight, to insult her, humiliate her. I didn't give a shit about her explanations; at that moment I was bent on never forgiving her again.

I rang the doorbell. The shrill voice of Laura, her sister, came out of the intercom.

"Who is it?"

"It's me, Manuel."

"Tania's not in," she said abruptly.

"Where'd she go?"

"I don't know. She left early."

There was a pause on the intercom. I didn't know if Laura was still there. I couldn't stand these gadgets.

"Laura?"

"What?"

"What time will she be back?"

"I'm not really sure . . . Anyway, see you later, I've got stuff to do."

"Laura," I shouted, so that she wouldn't leave.

"What?"

"I've got some things for Tania, can you open up so I can give them to you?"

"Come back later."

"I can't."

"All right, I'm coming."

She opened the door after making me wait for a long while. She was wearing khaki shorts, a blouse, and some sneakers.

"What are you going to give me?"

I raised my arms as if something had disappeared between them. She looked at me, annoyed.

"Stop being such a smart-ass, Manuel, I don't have time for this," she said and half-closed the door.

I held it with my forearm.

"Can I come in and wait for Tania?"

"No, I'm busy. Come back later, good-bye."

She tried to close the door, but I pushed back with my elbow.

"No, I'd prefer to wait."

"I'm alone and I won't be able to pay attention to you," she shot back grumpily. She seemed to do everything in a bad mood.

"I don't want you to pay attention to me," I said and went in. She slammed the door behind me.

I went into the living room and sat on a couch. She stared at me with her arms crossed.

"You're very aggressive, you know that?"

She looked nice in shorts. It pained me to admit it, but she had nicer legs than Tania.

"What do you mean?"

"I asked you not to come in."

There was a hint of surrender in her tone.

"I just want to wait for Tania."

"But I asked you not to come in," she repeated, this time in a better mood.

She seemed hurt, as if I'd just gravely humiliated her.

"What's wrong?" I asked, confused.

"Nothing, I just don't like it when you walk in here like you own the place."

"I'll leave if you want me to."

She shook her head and sat on the back of the couch.

"Keep doing whatever you were doing," I proposed. She didn't answer. She just stared at an ashtray in the middle of the coffee table.

Laura was a homely girl, attached to her parents. She was oppressed by Tania's personality, and the only way she could defend herself was by bitterly criticizing her. She especially disapproved of the fact that she was going out with her exboyfriend's best friend.

There was another reason: Gregorio had thought of Laura before Tania, but then found her to be inane. Laura considered their relationship to be an intimate, painful defeat, not because she was interested in Gregorio, but because her little sister had topped her again.

Once, while Tania was cooking dinner, I went upstairs to look for a book. When I went back down the hallway, Laura suddenly walked out of the bathroom stark naked. We were face-to-face. She neither shouted nor made an effort to cover herself. She remained quiet and still. I looked down at her body, her vehement breasts, her narrow hips, her curly, chestnut pubic hair. Laura remained static, following my eyes with hers. We were like this for forty, fifty seconds, until I decided to step around her. She walked past me, slowly. I looked back and watched her walk to her room.

We never said anything about it, and we acted as if nothing had ever happened. I'm sure that she considered those fifty seconds a victory: Somehow, by turning me on, she had managed to beat her sister.

After that encounter, Laura was a little less severe with me. Just a little.

"Do you want something to drink?" she suddenly asked.

"No, thanks," I said, "and, honestly, if you've got things to do, go do them."

She nodded, stood up, and walked up the stairs. I went to look for a book in the father's studio, but I only found legal manuals, bestsellers, and condensed Reader's Digest novels. I found a magazine on the desk and returned to the living room to look at it.

I couldn't concentrate on reading. Sometimes I felt furious, sometimes nervous. At any moment, Tania could appear and, even though I'd prepared a speech in my head, I probably wouldn't know what to say once I saw her.

I went into the kitchen to pour myself a glass of water, to calm down. As I walked past the stairs, I heard sobbing from the upper floor. I went up quietly and sat down on the last step to listen. Laura was on the phone with a friend, telling her how the boy she was dating had just broken up with her. She couldn't understand why.

Men always end up dumping Laura. Maybe it was because of her bad moods, her lack of personality, or maybe because she unconsciously pushed them to do so. She'd only had one boyfriend and they lasted three months. He was self-important, mean, and mistreated her. "That's what she gets for being so stupid and snooty," said Tania. I disagreed: Laura was shy and insecure, not a bad person.

While she was on the phone, Laura kept repeating "Why? Why?" She seemed afflicted. Her friend was probably trying to cheer her up by saying things like "Men are like that," or "It's not that bad—there are other men out there," or some such bullshit, but instead of calming down, Laura would sob even more intensely.

She hung up after fifteen minutes. I heard her blow her nose like a little girl. Some paternal impulse came upon me and I went to her room to console her.

The door was partially open. Laura was lying facedown on her bed, with her hair in a mess, barefoot, with one foot on top of the other, and with a Kleenex in her left hand. She moaned in irregular spasms. Like the woman in Doctor Macías's office, Laura seemed like a woman destined to give in, to sabotage herself. And at that moment I understood why men repudiated her. I turned around and went back to the living room.

TANIA'S PARENTS arrived an hour later. They were surprised by my presence.

"Tania said she was going to the movies with you," her mother explained.

"Yeah, but I had to finish some schoolwork and we said we'd meet here at nine," I lied.

Laura came downstairs dressed in shorts, and her father reprimanded her for it.

"Go change right now," he ordered.

"I'm old enough to decide what I wear," Laura protested.

"Not while you live in this house you don't."

The mother interceded and Laura got her way. Tania's father would randomly assume fake conservative opinions. I'm convinced he didn't give a damn about them, but they were a way to impose himself on his older daughter and, so, make up for Tania's rebelliousness.

He sat down to talk to me. I would have preferred for him to leave me alone—not because I thought he was boring, on the contrary, he was funny, but I wasn't interested in hearing about the details of corruption in arbitration procedures, on which he was an expert. Luckily, he received a phone call and let me be.

Later, the mother offered me dinner. I accepted and sat down at the table with her and Laura. For Tania's family, dinner had to be frugal. They gave me a plate with two helpings of cooked vegetables and a thin fillet of fried fish. I don't know why none of them were bone-thin.

The parents didn't consider me an ideal boyfriend for their daughter, even though they obviously preferred me to Gregorio. They tolerated me because they thought Tania was a problem child and that I somehow provided some stability. "That girl needs tough love," her father once said. He never gave it though, not because he didn't want to, but because Tania has known how to dominate him since she was a little girl. She was neither upset by his shouting nor affected by his scolding. She just ignored him and went somewhere else. In exchange, Laura would shrink before her father and bear his authoritarian abuses.

TANIA DIDN'T ARRIVE, and at eleven-thirty I decided to leave. We called a few of her friends and none of them had heard anything. As I left, the mother took me by the hand. "Help her," she said as she squeezed. "Help her, please."

When I arrived home my father was waiting for me.

"Why did you take your mother's car without asking?" he demanded.

"Something urgent came up."

"And that's why you didn't tell her?"

I shrugged my shoulders.

"Your mother had to meet her friends and had no way to get there."

"Sorry," I mumbled.

"She's the one you have to apologize to, and she's very angry."

"I'll talk to her tomorrow," I said.

My father shook his head and walked toward his bedroom. I went into mine and sat on the floor. Tania's absence was bothering me again. The speech I'd made, the insults, the jealous scene, they were stuck in my throat. I called Margarita. I was hoping that Tania would be parked outside of her house again.

"Hey," I said upon answering.

"Who's this?" she asked sleepily.

"Manuel."

She was quiet for a moment.

"I can't talk to you," she said.

"Why?"

"There's a big fight going on at the house."

"What happened?"

"I don't know how, but Joaquín found out about us."

"How?"

"I have no idea."

"And what did you say?"

"That it was a lie."

"Your parents know?"

"Uh-huh."

"And?"

"My dad was furious and so was Joaquín. They say it wasn't enough for you to fuck Gregorio's girlfriend."

"Deny it all."

"I assured them a hundred times that nothing happened between us, but they don't believe me."

"I think that . . ."

She interrupted me.

"Someone's coming, bye," she said and hung up.

Nobody could know about us. We were careful and discreet. I suspected that Jacinto Anaya was the snitch. But how could he know? I pulled out the card where I'd written down his phone number. I dialed slowly, making sure I dialed the right numbers. The phone rang four times and after the fifth, an answering machine answered. "I'm not home. Leave a message, name and number after the beep," ordered a raspy, male voice. I hung up.

Half an hour later I called again. The message started and I hung up. I did this over and over until, exasperated, at two AM, I left a message: "Jacinto Anaya, this is Manuel Aguilera. If you're so fucking tough, come drop the letters off in person. Give them to me face-to-face, you faggot, or are you afraid? If you've got something to say to me, say it to my face. My phone number is 635–00–19."

Angry, I slammed the phone down.

I was exhausted and fell asleep in my clothes with the light on. At four in the morning, the phone rang. The sound startled me.

"Hello."

"Tania isn't back yet," said Laura, on the other end of the line. "My mom's been crying all night," she added.

"You don't have any idea where she might be?" I asked.

"We know even less than you do."

She breathed in and went on.

"I don't know how you can go out with her, she's a real bitch."

I was surprised at her coarseness. She didn't usually talk like this.

"No, she's not."

"Don't defend her. What if she's fucking some other guy right now, and you don't even know about it?"

"Or maybe your ex-boyfriend is the one fucking other people?"

"That's none of your business," she scolded.

"It could be, don't you think?"

"Asshole," she yelled and hung up.

I WAS UNABLE TO SLEEP for the rest of the night. I felt hemmed in, confused, humiliated, jealous. And what if Laura was right? What the hell was Tania doing? Where the fuck had she gone?

My parents were asleep, so I couldn't look for my mother's sleeping pills. I wanted those pills like never before; I wanted to swallow the whole jar and be knocked out for a week.

The sun rose. I stayed in bed, wrapped in the covers, listening to the noises of the other life. I heard my father tiptoe out of the house, I heard my brother's alarm clock, I heard my mother walk downstairs, the maid sweep the patio, the racket made by the blender, the engine of the school bus as it picked up the twins from across the street. The other life.

At ten in the morning I decided to get up. I opened the window, the air was warm, the sky transparent. I went downstairs for breakfast. My mother was dicing some vegetables on the kitchen table. She gave me a sidelong glance.

"Aren't you going to school?" she asked.

"Later," I answered.

She made a gesture of disgust and continued with her task. When I started college, I took a psychological exam—a written questionnaire where you could only answer yes, no, or don't know. One of the questions was "Do you get along well with your mother?" It took me fifteen minutes to choose. I marked "yes" without much conviction when I should've answered "don't know."

I made myself some scrambled eggs with ham and ate them sitting across from her, without talking, both of us focused on our own things. And I didn't apologize for having taken her car.

I WENT BACK TO MY ROOM to try to sleep. It was hot. I got naked, unplugged the phone, lay facedown, and closed my eyes. I was beginning to dream when I felt an earwig running up my back. I rolled over on the mattress, trying to crush it, and I sat up to try to shake it off. I pulled the sheets off the bed and scrutinized it carefully. Again, nothing.

Despite the heat, I put on the blue flannel pajamas and covered myself with the blankets. That way, I thought, I'd be better protected. I managed to sleep for two, three hours, until I was awoken by someone knocking on the door.

"Who is it?" I asked.

"Someone on the phone," said my mother angrily and walked away.

I picked up the receiver.

"Hello."

"Manuel?"

"Yeah."

"Do you know who this is?"

"No."

"Jacinto Anaya."

Stunned, I was quiet for a few moments.

"What do you want?" I asked.

"What do you want?"

"I want you to stop fucking with me."

"I don't even know you," he said.

We remained silent. His voice was deeper, more masculine than it was on his answering machine. It matched neither his pudgy figure nor his bland calligraphy.

"If you don't know me, then stop sending me letters and stupid fucking little notes," I shot back furiously.

"We need to talk, don't you think?" he said.

"If you're not afraid," I said.

"I'll be waiting for you at five, at the zoo, by the jaguar pit. I guess you know where it is, right?" he said ironically.

"Yes."

He didn't say anything else and hung up. To meet me specifically at the jaguar pit seemed like a declaration of war. He knew more about me than I'd imagined. I tried to call him back to curse at him, but first the line was busy, and then the answering machine picked up.

AT THREE IN THE AFTERNOON I showered, got dressed, and took the gun Camariña had given me out of the drawer. I didn't really know who Jacinto Anaya was, whether he was a dangerous psychotic or just an idiot playing the wrong game.

I put on a wool sweater—an absurd item of clothing for such a hot day, but baggy enough to hide the bulk of the revolver in my waist.

With a gun, I couldn't use a taxi or public transport. I needed my mom's car. I looked for the keys, but she'd hidden them. There was no choice but to ask her. Of course, she refused. I claimed it was urgent. She refused again.

"I really need it."

"So do I."

"Not as much as I do."

"How do you know?" she said, annoyed. She got up and closed the door to her room.

I remembered my father kept duplicates in a corner of the laundry room. I looked in every nook and cranny but couldn't find them. I never paid attention when he explained that that was where he kept them for emergencies.

Resigned, I went outside to wait for a taxi. I finally found one after half an hour. It was hot as hell inside the car, but I didn't dare take off the sweater. I opened the window and reclined on the seatback. The taxi was driving too slowly between the other vehicles. The heat made me dizzy. I closed my eyes and the image of Rebecca's white torso came to mind—just her torso, naked, without a face, moist, stretching out after making love. I opened my eyes. The cars were moving slowly. The exasperated drivers were staring dead ahead, a woman was scolding some kid, a truck driver was dabbing at his sweat with a handkerchief, and a white body was being unveiled in my memory, a body I'd never again caress, kiss, smell. I missed Rebecca, her white torso, her silent orgasms. I missed her peace, her serenity. Her serenity.

I made sure the revolver was safe at my hip, closed my eyes again, and fell asleep.

· · ·

WE MADE IT TO THE ZOO after almost an hour. The driver woke me up with a "Here we are." I sat up. The meter read forty-two pesos. I paid with a fifty-peso bill—the only one I had in my wallet. The taxi driver gave me my change in fifty-cent coins.

I asked the guy what time it was. Ten to five. Time had passed quickly. I stood before the zoo gates. The people strolled aimlessly, a few salesmen were hawking their wares, a couple was kissing. I gulped and went in.

I walked decisively toward the jaguar pit. Halfway there I felt something missing on my left. I stopped and turned around: the cage with the ochre coyote was empty. I walked up to it. There was just a fistful of dry shit stacked in a corner and a gnawed horse bone. I asked one of the employees what had happened.

"It died," he answered.

"What of?"

"Who knows? Kids throw all sorts of crap in there. One day a hippopotamus died and when they opened its belly they found a baseball glove, and a javelina had a baby bottle . . ."

I looked back at the cage. I remembered the coyote trotting in circles, intense, alive.

"You should be more careful . . ."

"We try, we try," he said with the verbiage of a bureaucrat.

"Bullshit 'you try,'" I said and left.

I REACHED THE FELINE AREA and slowed down. I stealthily approached, trying to spot Jacinto Anaya before he spotted me. I arrived at the pit and there was nobody there. As usual, the two jaguars were lying there, inert, twirling their tails every now and again.

I walked a few meters away and sat on a bench under the shade of a large tree. From there I could watch people approach the pit from the two paths that led to it.

Minutes went by. A woman in a gray uniform started to sweep behind me. I moved so she wouldn't cover me in dust, and looked for somewhere else to sit. I suddenly saw Tania walking down one of the paths. I hid behind a tree trunk. She stopped in front of the pit, looked around, took a cigarette out of her purse, lit it and watched the jaguars.

I watched her for a while. She was smoking worriedly. I saw her make gestures that I'd never seen before: how she blew out the smoke, how she bit her nails, how she lifted her chin toward the sun. She seemed like a stranger, a woman unknown and distant. I felt a sense of uneasiness, a clawing at my stomach. I couldn't wait any longer and I walked up to her.

"What are you doing here?" I asked her.

She turned around, looked at me surprised and immediately flicked the cigarette away (she had promised she would never smoke in front of me after she found out that my grandmother had died of pulmonary emphysema).

"What are you doing here?" she asked, disturbed.

"I came looking for you."

"How did you know I was coming?"

"Every time you get lost, I come here to look for you."

"You know me well," she said with a half-smile, nervous. She moistened her lips and sighed lengthily.

"I missed you a lot," she said.

I shook my head. "That's not true."

"Why don't you believe me?"

"Because if you'd missed me you would have come give me a kiss."

"You scared me," she said. She hugged me and kissed me on the mouth.

"Were you expecting anyone else?" I asked.

"No, why?"

"Because I was."

"A new girlfriend?" she joked.

"No, a friend. Maybe you know him: Jacinto Anaya."

Upon hearing Jacinto's name, Tania looked away, at where the male jaguar was sleeping.

"They're pretty, aren't they?"

"They bore me."

"Why?"

"They don't move; they don't do any tricks."

Tania brushed the hair away from her face and smiled. That was the expression she made that I liked the most, and she knew it. It was her way of seducing me, of alleviating the tension.

"That's what I admire about them the most: that they lie there for most of the day, but they just need a second to kill."

Tania looked back at the pit and pointed at the male.

"Look at them. They're the most beautiful animals on the planet."

I looked around to make sure Jacinto Anaya wasn't there. I grabbed Tania by the arm and pulled her. She thought I was doing it to kiss her. She prepared her lips, but I avoided her.

"What's wrong with you?" she asked.

"How do you know Jacinto Anaya?" I asked her, squeezing her arm.

"I don't know who he is," she answered and tried to break free.

"Don't bullshit me," I shouted and squeezed even harder.

The woman who was sweeping stopped and watched us.

"Don't make one of your scenes," warned Tania.

I let go of her and she rubbed her arm. She rummaged through her purse, took out another cigarette and lit it.

"They're the most beautiful animals," she repeated, staring at the pit.

"How do you know him," I insisted.

Tania gave the cigarette another long drag and exhaled as she tilted her head. Another unknown gesture.

"I told you I don't know who he is," she answered, irritated.

We remained silent. She leaned her forehead on the chain-link fence. Her hair shone in the sun.

"Where were you last night?"

She turned to look at me with an annoyed expression on her face.

"At Claudine Longega's."

"No you weren't," I refuted.

"Of course I was."

"Laura called her and Claudine said she didn't know where you were."

Tania smiled sarcastically.

"Don't believe everything my retarded sister says."

"I was next to her when she called."

Tania looked annoyed again.

"Enough, come on, get off my back," she said and brought her cigarette up to her mouth.

I slapped the cigarette out of her lips. It flew off and landed in the gutter that separated the pit from the fence.

"It pisses me off when you smoke," I bellowed.

Tania looked at me indignantly, her eyes brimming with tears.

"Why?" she asked and lowered her head. "Why do you have to know everything?"

She brought her left hand to her face and tears started to roll down her cheeks. I grabbed her shoulders and pulled her toward me.

"Just answer this question. I'm not asking anything else. In these last months, how many times did you sleep with Gregorio?"

"None," she whispered.

"Stop lying, goddammit!"

Tania raised her hands, put them against my chest, and pushed me backward.

"None," she repeated.

She wiped away her tears, clenched her teeth, and turned around to leave. I jumped in her way.

"Look in my fucking eyes, look at me and for once in your life tell me the truth, I'm asking you, please."

Tania clicked her tongue and shook her head.

"Gregorio doesn't matter anymore."

"Tell me the truth."

She looked me in the eyes and lifted her face defiantly.

"You don't deserve it."

"Oh, no?"

"No."

She made another attempt to leave, but I blocked her way. She wasn't crying anymore.

"Tell me."

"I slept with him about five times less than you slept with Margarita," she confessed.

Her revelation incensed me.

"I never slept with Margarita," I affirmed, "and you did sleep with Gregorio, you fucking slut."

"So now it's your turn to lie?" she asked sardonically.

"It's not a lie, for fuck's sake!"

Tania arched her eyebrows and stared right at me.

"Enough bullshit, don't you think?"

I started to feel I was losing control and I pulled her by the blouse.

"You fucking slut, you fucking slut!" I screamed.

Tania stepped forward and hit me on the jaw with the back of her hand.

"We're even, you bastard."

I pulled out the gun and Tania stepped back, frightened.

"What are you doing?" she asked.

"You're a whore!" I yelled.

I shot into the air. The woman who was sweeping threw herself on the ground and covered her head with her arms. Tania looked at me, stunned.

"What are you doing?" she repeated fearfully.

I wanted to control myself, to throw the gun into the trees and dominate myself, but I just couldn't.

I turned to the pit and started to shoot at the male jaguar. The first shot hit him in his shanks. The jaguar got up unsteadily and started to turn in a circle. I adjusted my aim and the second and third shot hit him in the chest. The jaguar roared in pain and writhed on the ground. I emptied the rest of the chamber at the cat without hitting him again.

The jaguar's roars were deafening. A guard started to blow his whistle. Tania and I looked at each other.

"I'm sorry," I muttered.

The whistles became increasingly close and I ran. I jumped some shrubs and headed as fast as I could toward the exit. A guard tried to stop me and I ran over him. I realized I'd never reach the gates. I jumped over the kids' choo-choo train tracks and climbed over the fence that surrounded the park with the revolver still in hand. I fell on the other side and I ran and I ran. People moved aside when they saw me. As I was running I spotted a cracked manhole and I threw the gun in. I was sweating. The wool sweater made my neck and back itch. And with every step I was sweating even more.

I crossed Reforma Avenue, dodging the cars, then cut through the Museum of Anthropology's parking lots and then I ran into Polanco. I ran for blocks and blocks until I burst. I stepped behind the wall of an abandoned lot and dropped onto a mound of grass. I was scared of myself, and regretful. I thought the police wouldn't stop until they found me, and that dozens of patrol cars would be hot on my trail.

I took off the sweater. The sweat was soaking my back and my chest. The itch from the wool was unbearable. My legs were shaking. I was having trouble breathing. I sunk my face in the grass. I couldn't understand why I'd done it. I started to cry as if I were crying out somebody else's pain, until it got dark.

I LAY ON THE GRASS for four or five hours. Tired, very tired. I felt as if time was slipping, not going by. The lights looked dull, the noises silent: fake. All fake. Set design.

A family of mice ran back and forth in front of me. Three large mice and four small ones went in and out of some discarded shelves. Seven gray ghosts. I wanted to kill one, gut it, and leave it to rot in the night's heat. What do dead mice smell like? Did Tania know? Tania, Tania. I was rotting in the heat of the night and so were the jaguar's wounds. What does it smell like between a woman's legs? Does it smell like dead mice? Or treachery? Does it smell like Gregorio, or does it smell like me? What the fuck does it smell like?

I thought and thought and didn't move, staring at the mice, facedown, waiting for the world, in its turning, to fix what I had messed up. And I didn't move, thinking . . . thinking, while the mice slipped past me, nervous, vigilant.

I managed to get up and sat on the mound of grass. The mice fled. I could glimpse them in their nest, but they wouldn't come out anymore. I decided that the best thing I could do was hide in room 803. I went out into the street. Even though the subway station was close by, I decided to take a taxi. I asked the driver to take me to Pirineos Street, in the Portales neighborhood. I opened the window so the wind would hit me in the face. I thought of Tania. I didn't want to lose her. I loved her too much, dammit, too much.

The meter progressively read fifteen, twenty, twenty-five, thirty pesos. I put my hand in my pants pocket and pulled out the fistful of fifty-cent coins I still had. When, approaching a stoplight, the taxi slowed down, I threw the coins on the front seat, jumped out, and ran down a side street, against the traffic. I managed to hear the cabdriver cursing at me.

I arrived at the motel. Pancho was watching TV in his office sitting on a stool.

"Hey," I said.

"Hey," he answered.

It was a relief to see him. The dark-skinned guy had gotten sick and Camariña had asked Pancho to cover for him. At least he'd be around for the night.

I stayed and watched TV for a while. Pancho knew all the intricacies of the soap opera we were watching, and during the commercials he'd explain the basic plot. It was about a chick who was trying to decide whether she should continue her relationship with a married man who loved her madly, or break up with him to go live in a village by the sea. According to Pancho, the girl still hadn't decided after a hundred episodes, and by the looks of things, it would take her another hundred to do so.

Once the episode ended, there was a news bulletin. News about a presidential tour, a new law to help promote foreign investment, the arrest of some car thieves. Nothing about the zoo.

Pancho informed me that Tania hadn't been to the motel. "There haven't been any clients," he lamented, "it's really boring." He offered me some of the chicken tacos his mother had prepared for him (were they the equivalent of my chicken sandwiches?). When he finished eating, he excused himself and left to put a new load of sheets into the washing machine. His departure weighed on me.

I headed toward the room. In the hallway I bumped into the guy with the curly hair. He greeted me affectionately, as if there were a long-standing friendship between us. He stopped to chat, and in twenty minutes had already told me about his alcoholic father, his sister's marriage to a Canadian, his nephew's excellent grades in primary school, and gave me a description of his great grandfather. I would've liked for him to go on and on until dawn, for him to keep me company, but a couple showed up in a white Jetta and he went to collect their money.

The room was impeccable. They'd changed the old comforter for a new one and you could smell the tile cleaner. Eusebio Ruvalcaba's novel was still on the nightstand, still open to the page at which I'd left it.

I lay naked on the new comforter. I didn't know what would happen, if I'd see Tania again, if I'd hear from Jacinto, if I'd be free of Gregorio and his destruction. It suddenly seemed ridiculous: the letters, Tania's disappearances, the mystery of Jacinto, the revealed secrets, the wounded jaguar, myself.

I picked up Ruvalcaba's novel. Oralia, a friend, had shown me a way to use any book as if it were the *I Ching*. You had to ask a question, then open the book at random and read the fifth sentence from the third paragraph. You had to scratch dialogue, pages written in less than three paragraphs, and, obviously, paragraphs written in less than five sentences.

"What's happening?" I asked. I flipped through the book and stopped on page eighty-one. It said: "Everyone was telling his own version." It seemed like a punctual synthesis of what was going on around me. There were too many versions of one story, and instead of making the story clearer, they made it more confusing. Gregorio was ferociously telling his version, Tania ran from hers, Margarita was burdened by hers, and I was looking for mine.

"What's going to happen?" was my second question. It landed on page nineteen. It said: "And the soldier was awaiting death as one awaits the sunrise." It felt like a terrible premonition. Who was waiting for death? I was scared and closed the book. I turned out the lights but couldn't get to sleep: I was afraid of facing the night, the long night of the blue buffalo.

I left the room for some air. I found Pancho sleeping on a couch in the office. I looked for the guy with the curly hair so we could chat, but couldn't find him. I went around the back of the reception and walked down the corridor that ran behind the rooms toward the laundry. He was ducking under the window of room 804, spying on the couple in the white Jetta through a sliver between the curtains. I noticed he was masturbating. Intimacy turned peep show. The number of times the bastard must've spied on us! I felt pity for him and, disgusted, returned to the room.

• • •

EXHAUSTION OVERCAME ME. When I opened my eyes it was ten in the morning. I put my pants on and went out onto the patio. Pancho was washing the floor of one of the driveways, in a good mood, as usual. I asked him if he had bought any newspapers for that day, so I could borrow one. He went into the office and brought out *Reforma*. I sat down to read it on the carpet. A column on the first page told of the death of a jaguar at the hands of a "madman." There was more information in the City section. The reporter began the article with "a bullet fired in the heart of the afternoon cut short the life of one of the most majestic animals at Chapultepec Zoo." She then went on to tell of a scene where a girl was about to be mugged by "a lunatic, who, upon failing in his attempt, unleashed his rage by shooting at the jaguar point-blank." Several witnesses corroborated this, including, of course, the woman who was sweeping around the pit.

A VETERINARY DOCTOR specified that the jaguar had died from respiratory arrest caused by a hemorrhage in his right lung. "He died asphyxiated by his own blood," the reporter concluded.

Other articles reported various reactions. The zoo director found the act to be "aberrant and cruel." An assembly member wanted "severe punishment" and a member of the opposition assured that "this lamentable occurrence derived from the inefficiency of city authorities to contain urban violence."

I turned the page. At the top was an artist's sketch of the criminal. The image looked nothing like my face. Tania had de cided to make a brilliant, subtle move: She had described Gregorio, and the artist had managed an almost perfect likeness. I laughed out loud. Surely the judicial police had distributed the portrait to all its agents. I imagined them investigating a suspect who had died a week earlier, following leads all the way to his urn.

There was no doubt: Tania played in the major leagues. She was too much woman and I couldn't lose her, especially now that, from the pages of a newspaper, she was mocking Gregorio and sending me proof of her love.

I WENT TO RECEPTION to use the phone. I needed to call home to tell them I was okay. My brother answered. He warned me that my father was very angry about the fact that I hadn't been home. I said that I had had a last-minute, urgent school project, and that I had no choice but to meet my schoolmates at one of their houses. "Make that clear to dad," I requested. I asked him if there were any messages. He said that, in the morning, a tall fat man had come around looking for me. Luis asked what he could do for him, and the fat man gave him two letters and added: "Tell Manuel that I brought them personally so that he knows I don't hide, and also tell him that what he did yesterday afternoon was very, very bad." Luis had left the letters in my room. That was it, and we hung up.

The fat man's visit made me feel vulnerable. He apparently had seen what happened in the zoo and could blackmail me. He had probably seen everything, spying on Tania and me like the guy with the curly hair had spied on the couple in the motel. Piece-of-shit voyeurs, the both of them.

I called information to try to find out what address matched his telephone number, but the operator said Jacinto had a private number and she was unable to tell me any more.

I dialed Jacinto's house and the machine answered. "Fuck you, motherfucker," I yelled into the phone and hung up. I called Tania's house to see if she'd been back. Between sobs, her mother informed me that she hadn't. She had a feeling something terrible had happened to her daughter. I tried to calm her, assuring her Tania would be back any moment. Her mother kept sobbing, so I decided to say good-bye.

On the reception desk was a packet of spicy peanuts. I stole it. I didn't have any money for breakfast or to get back home. I regretted throwing all my coins at the taxi driver.

I went to the room and sat on the bed to eat the peanuts. Fifteen minutes later I heard the sound of a car parking in the driveway. I looked out: a red Cavalier. Maybe an absentminded couple had driven into our garage. Pancho would sort out the mix-up.

I took my clothes off and got in the shower. The water falling on my back relaxed me. I wanted to remain calm, with enough clarity to avoid another mistake like the one in the zoo.

I finished showering, dried off, and wrapped myself in a towel. When I walked out of the bathroom I found Tania sitting on the bed, staring at me fixedly. Without saying a word, she got up, walked toward me, undid the knot holding my towel up, and took it off. She took a step back, looked at me naked, then grabbed my hand and led me toward the bed.

"Hug me," she said.

"No."

She moved close to me and I pulled away. Tania let herself drop onto the mattress and lay there with her arms open.

"You're not coming?"

I shook my head. Tania sighed and turned her back to me.

"We have to talk," I said.

"There's nothing to talk about," she muttered.

I sat on the opposite edge of the bed. Tania turned around and fixed her gaze on me again.

"I missed you," she said.

She got up and started to unbutton her blouse.

"You didn't have to kill him," she said.

"I didn't want to."

"He was roaring like crazy, then stayed still, coughing blood, until he didn't move anymore . . ."

She stopped for a moment, bit her nail and went on.

"I wanted to get out of there, but I couldn't stop looking at it . . . I couldn't . . . then a bunch of people arrived, and the police."

She crumpled up her blouse into a ball and threw it onto the chair. She took off her bra and her breasts were exposed.

"Can you imagine if one day they found a tumor and I had to have them removed?"

"Don't talk shit."

She brought her hands to her breasts and squeezed them hard.

"Can you imagine my chest empty, full of stitches?"

Tania knew how to be cruel when she wanted to.

"I can't imagine it," I answered.

She let go of her breasts and her fingers were imprinted on her skin. She got rid of the rest of her clothes and got between the sheets.

"Come," she insisted.

I looked at her without answering.

"Please, come . . ."

"We have to talk," I repeated.

"Later," she requested.

I lay down next to her; she kissed me and stroked my forehead.

"I love you much more than you think," she said.

"I don't believe you," I said.

She tried to kiss me on the mouth. I squeezed my lips together and pushed her chin away with my index finger.

"I can't," I said.

She looked me in the eyes.

"All this is hurting me, too. I'm hurt by what you did, I'm hurt by what I did."

She tried to kiss me again, but I eluded her.

"I can't, and I don't want to," I said.

She took my face in both her hands and pulled up close to me.

"Hold me for ten minutes, please, that's all I'm asking. If you want to you can kick me out later, spit on me, beat me up, whatever the hell you want. But right now hold me."

We made love with a sad intensity. When we finished, Tania pushed my penis out and started to pee with a slow, continuous flow. I felt her urine slide down my stomach and between my thighs, warm, thick. "Golden showers," she mumbled.

I hugged her with strength. I wanted to be impregnated with her, soaked in her urine, her sweat, her saliva, her vaginal juices. I never loved as much as her at that moment. I didn't want to fight with her anymore. Her relationship with Gregorio, her disappearances, her secrets, were diluted in the loving torrent of her urine. What did it matter if Gregorio had penetrated her a dozen times? That was the end of him. Tania leaned her head against my chest, without talking.

"What are you thinking about?" I asked her.

She sighed and smiled.

"Our kids," she answered, "what they'd be like, what we'd call them."

"What would they be like?" I asked.

She kissed me on the forehead and remained pensive for a long time.

"They're going to fail me in all my courses this semester," she suddenly said.

"You go one day and skip ten, what did you expect?"

"So, what's better, quality or quantity?"

She laughed a little at her joke and was quiet again. Her naked body shimmered slightly.

"I swear I've been sleeping at Claudine's house these days," she explained out of the blue.

"Then why did she say she didn't know where you were?"

"I asked her to."

"Why?"

She kept silent for a few seconds and then went on:

"She lent me her car to come here; mine got stuck a few blocks away from her house. I'm so stupid. I always forget to put gas in it."

She got up and kneeled next to me. She studied my features and her face lit up.

"I know!" she exclaimed, "if it's a boy, I want him to look like me and if it's a girl, like you."

"Poor girl," I joked.

She leaned over me, grabbed her bag from the nightstand, and took out a watch. She looked at the time and jumped off the bed.

"It's really late, I've got to go."

"Don't go," I implored.

"I need to give Claudine her car back or she'll kill me."

"Bring it back later."

"I can't, but I promise I'll come back as soon as possible."

"Promise?"

"I swear." She headed to the bathroom and stopped in the middle of the room. "Aren't you coming to take a shower?" she asked.

"No, I want to smell like you for the rest of the day."

She smiled and blew me a kiss. I sunk my face in the pillow. We should buy a TV, we should change the curtains, hang up some more paintings, bring more books, a radio. We should move into room 803 and never leave it.

I got hungry. I took Tania's bag and rummaged through it in search of something to eat. I found a tube of LifeSavers and popped a lemon one in my mouth. I opened her wallet to see if she had enough money so she could lend me some. Among the bills, I found two pieces of paper, folded in fours. I opened them and spread them out on the bed. On both were written, in Gregorio's hand, lyrics from pop songs. On one he'd written: "At night I only hear the beat of our love." On the other: "How can I forget the embers of your love, / how can I stand the night without your skin . . ."

I kept looking through her bag and I found an envelope with Jacinto Anaya's handwriting on it. On the front he'd written "Tania," below it, "January 20th." Inside was a paper napkin on which Gregorio had scrawled an unfinished phrase: "I'll wait, I'll wait for you on . . ."

I put everything back in the bag. I closed it and put it back on the nightstand. My head hurt and I was out of breath. Again, the jealousy, the fear of losing her, Gregorio's goddamn ghost interfering, hurting, destroying.

I heard Tania turn off the water. How to face her? What to

say to her? She opened the door and a billow of steam escaped into the room. Tania walked out naked, with her wet hair dripping on her body. She stood in front of the mirror and looked at her profile.

"I need a tan," she said.

She sat on the edge of the bed and asked me to dry her hair. I knelt behind her and rubbed her head with a towel. Tania allowed it, docile, loose. I was suddenly overcome by the anxiety of not knowing who she really was or where she was going. As if she had read my mind, she turned around and kissed me on the lips.

"I'll never stop loving you," she said.

"Are you sure?"

"Positive . . ."

She stood up, dried the back of her neck and picked up her clothes.

SHE STARTED TO GET DRESSED distractedly, as if she were alone in the room. I always liked to watch her do it, but this time there was a knot in my throat.

Tania bent over, threw her hair over her head and brushed it several times. Some drops of water sprinkled on the carpet. Tania stood up, fixed her hair with her hands, looked at herself in the mirror one more time, and sat down next to me.

"I'll be back in one or two hours," she said.

"Sure."

She looked at me for a few seconds and ran her index finger over my face.

"Good-bye," she said and got up. I grabbed her by the arm.

"We need to talk when you get back," I told her.

She looked at the floor and shook her head.

"It's not worth it."

"It is to me."

"No . . ."

"We have a lot to clear up," I interrupted her.

"Forget it."

"Please, I need to," I insisted.

She bit her lips and agreed. She kissed me for a long time and then left. I heard her get into the car and start the engine. Then I heard the car door open again. I got up and heard a noise at the door. Tania slipped a piece of paper under the door and then I heard her get back in the car. I looked out the window and managed to see the red Cavalier drive toward the exit.

ON THE PIECE OF PAPER, Tania had written: "It's at the end of the rainbow, / Where the golden showers are."

It was a quote from a Bukowski poem, where he writes about a man's true happiness at being peed on by a baby while he changes his diaper.

On the back of the sheet, Tania had written: "Forgive me for what I did and for what I'm going to do." And under it: "I love you more than you think."

Tania was probably right: Why talk, why dwell on a past that couldn't be avoided? Better to accept the facts and forgive them. Better to forgive than to lose her.

I doubled over my stomach to smell her. My pubic hair was still damp from her urine. I put her short letter on the pillow, lay down on it, and closed my eyes.

• • •

Two hours later, I was awoken by knocking at the door. Certain that it was Tania, I opened the door, wrapped in a towel, without looking through the keyhole. I encountered two men: one thin and of medium height, the other tall and burly.

"Manuel Aguilera?" asked the thin one.

I nodded.

"Please get dressed and come with us."

"Where?"

"You'll see."

"Just a moment," I said and pushed the door closed. I quickly put on my pants and shirt. I thought of jumping out the window, but through the curtain I could see two men guarding the hallway. I was sure Jacinto Anaya had ratted me out to the police.

I partially opened the door and asked the thin one if they could wait for me to have a shower.

"No," he said firmly, "and hurry up."

He didn't let me close the door again. I sat on the carpet and started to put my socks on. Pancho and Camariña walked up to the room.

"What's going on?" asked Camariña.

"Nothing," answered the thin guy.

Camariña looked into the room.

"What's happening, kid?" he asked me.

I shrugged my shoulders.

"I don't know."

I finished tying my shoelaces and left the room. The two men flanked me and led me to a white Spirit. Camariña got in the way.

"You can't just take him like this," he exclaimed.

Without getting upset, the stronger man asked him to step out of the way. Camariña insisted.

"Do you have a warrant?"

"Are you his relative?" asked the cop.

"No."

"Then please let us do our job," said the thin man courteously.

They opened the back door of the car and ordered me to sit in the middle. The other two cops appeared and sat on either side of me. Camariña still made one last attempt:

"Let him go and we'll find some way to sort this out ourselves," he proposed.

The burly man smiled mockingly, got into the driver's seat and buckled his seat belt.

"Good afternoon," he said and accelerated.

FOR MOST OF THE TRIP, the cops didn't talk. Every now and again, a woman's voice would come on their radio under the dashboard. I deduced the thin one was the boss by the way the others spoke to him. They didn't look like judicial police. They were wearing light suits, well tailored, well matched. They didn't threaten me, they weren't rude or aggressive. They just ignored me.

For some security reason, they kept their windows closed. They didn't seem to mind the suffocating heat. They remained impassive, focused on their thoughts.

Inside that heat, the smell of Tania emanating from my body became more concentrated, more pungent. It felt almost as if she were in the car. The entire air belonged to her. I don't know if the others perceived the smell of urine the same way I did, but it made me dizzy. I wanted to ask them to lower the windows so the car could get some ventilation, but I didn't dare.

I wasn't fully conscious of what was going on until I arrived at the precinct for the judicial police. The car drove into an underground parking lot and stopped in front of some elevators. The thin man and two other cops escorted me, while the strong cop drove away in the car.

We got in the elevator and rode it to the second floor. In the hallways, other agents greeted the thin man with deference, and he gave orders in a soft voice, to which they'd answer with a "yes, sir." We arrived at some offices. A secretary stood up when she saw us walk in and gave the thin man several documents. He leaned on the desk, read some papers, and signed some others. When he was finished, he led me into a small cubicle. He invited me in with an almost feminine gesture and asked me to wait for a moment. I went in and they left me alone. Through the blinds I could see that the two men who escorted me had stayed to guard me.

The cubicle was only furnished with a table and chair. It wasn't comfortable, but at least it wasn't a cell. Outside I could hear the continual ring of telephones and the chatter of typewriters. I looked through the window. Men in suits were resting on white Spirits. A bootblack was waiting for customers, sitting on a bench. Two women with their hair dyed blond were arguing vehemently. Some boys were playing hopscotch on the sidewalk. Everything went on the same, except me.

I was alone for a long time. At first I got very nervous, but as time passed, I began to calm down. I had committed several crimes: illegal possession of a firearm, damages to the nation, attempted robbery, etcetera. The most common crimes in tabloids. It wouldn't be easy to avoid the charges.

I once heard a man say, "In crime and love affairs, if you're caught, deny it all, even if your wife catches you with your pants down, or a cop sees you with a pistol in your fist, no pun intended . . ." He was bragging about having robbed several banks and having fucked dozens of women. He'd been caught a number of times, but he always found a way to walk. I met him because one of Tania's father's partners was his lawyer and one night we were at the same restaurant. With the presumption of an amateur, after ten minutes the man had told me his entire criminal and sex life. He didn't care who I was or what I did. To console myself, I thought that if a guy like that wasn't spending forty years in jail, I would surely be okay.

I was getting bored inside the cubicle and after three hours, I didn't know what to do with myself. I'd counted the knots in the carpet, calculated how many years I could get in jail, imagined the stories of all the cops outside the building: which one was a drug dealer, which one was gay, how many people they must have killed.

The thin man's delay began to worry me. What was taking so long? Was he preparing my file? Or corroborating the other witnesses' testimonies? I even came to think he'd forgotten about me.

I had to pee. I opened the door and asked one of the cops for permission to go the bathroom.

"Hold it a little longer," said my custodian like a primary school teacher.

That "little longer" went on for another three hours. At dusk, the thin man arrived with the strong cop. He apologized for the wait and ordered one of the guards to bring him a chair.

The thin guy sat before me and put a manila folder on the table.

"We haven't been officially introduced," he said with a smirk, "because I know that you're Manuel Aguilera, but you don't know who I am, right?"

I nodded and he held out his hand and shook mine.

"I'm Commander Martín Ramírez and this," he said, signaling the burly officer, "is Agent Luis Vives."

His cordiality was such that I was about to say "Pleased to meet you," or "Charmed," but I just said "Okay."

The thin man leaned back in his chair, put his palms together and brought them to his lips, as if he were about to pray.

"You know why you're here, right, Manuel?"

"No," I answered hesitantly.

"Come on, man! It's not good to lie."

"Really, I don't know what you're talking about."

The thin man turned to look at the strong man and smiled knowingly.

"How do you like our friend here?" he asked.

"Like Pinocchio," answered Vives.

"Yeah, that's right," he responded, "like Pinocchio."

He turned to look at me quizzically.

"But you're not Pinocchio, are you?"

"No."

"Phew, I thought I had the wrong person," he mocked.

From one of his suit pockets, he took out a pack of cigarettes, put one in his mouth and offered me another from the pack.

"No thanks," I said.

"Good for you," he said, "these things'll kill ya."

He lit it and exhaled the smoke toward the ceiling, the same way Camariña did.

"What team do you support?" he suddenly asked.

"Atlante."

"Hey, the workingman's team, the iron colts. Good, good. What d'you think about Rolossi?"

"The player?"

"Who else?"

"He's really good."

The thin guy received my answer with a smile and turned to look at Vives in complicity.

"See how you're lying: Rolossi's terrible."

"I don't think so," I answered back.

Again, they looked at each other.

"He's not just a liar, he's insolent, too. But anyway, we're not here to talk about soccer, are we?"

"I don't know why we're here."

The thin man rested his chin on his right fist.

"You don't?" he inquired, amazed.

"No."

He leaned toward me until his face was an inch away from mine. The smell of his menthol cigarettes made my nose itch.

"If you hadn't gone crazy at the zoo yesterday, you wouldn't be here," he explained.

"What zoo?"

He got up, walked around the table and stood behind me.

"Oh Pinocchio, Pinocchio! When are you going to stop lying?"

He walked back to his spot and leaned on his chair again.

"Are you always like this?" he asked with a smile.

"Not at all," I answered, trying to look as firm as possible.

The commander signaled for Vives to come closer. He whispered something in his ear and Vives left the cubicle.

"Let's see if you like this, just the two of us, you have a little more trust in me and tell me the truth."

His attitude was so relaxed that I worked up some courage.

"What am I accused of?" I asked.

"Pinocchio, Pinocchio, are you fucking with me?"

"I have the right to a phone call, don't I?"

"Four if you want, or more, twenty, thirty, a hundred."

"I want to tell my parents I'm here."

"Sure, but all in due time."

"I want to do it right now."

He stood up, walked over to me, lowered his face till his eyes were level with mine, and whispered:

"Listen, kid: I think there are some things that you haven't understood. I'm the one in charge here, and if you keep acting like a brat right now, I'll have them punch your balls till they burst, understand?" He said this with a little smile that intimidated me. He ran his fingers through his hair and went on:

"I'm tired, I've been working like crazy all day and I want to go home and watch TV and have a little fuck with my wife, because God knows I need it. I'll ask you questions, you tell me the truth, I'll be real happy, I'll fuck off home, and just from the sheer joy, I'll lend you the phone so you can call whoever the hell you want, deal?"

His offer was tempting. Maybe it was best to end this farce once and for all. But in my head all I could hear were the words *deny it all, deny it.*

"I'm telling you the truth: I don't know what you're talking about."

The thin man sighed, annoyed, and sat down again.

"Look Pinocchio, let me tell you: Yesterday evening, some guy lost his marbles and started shooting at the tigers like a psycho . . ."

"Jaguars," I was about to say, but I managed to catch my mistake just before I made it.

". . . the point is, this guy who felt he was hunting tigers in Africa . . ."

Again, I wanted to correct him: "There are no tigers in Africa."

". . . his aim was so good that he killed one, didn't you know؟"

I shook my head.

"Well, I think you do know," he said with conviction.

"Why؟"

"Because a female witness identified you as the valiant big-game hunter."

"A what . . . ؟" I asked.

"A witness, one of your fans, Indiana Jones."

It was a trap into which I could not fall: Jacinto Anaya had turned me in, no one else.

"Well, she must've been confused," I countered.

"Little Pinocchio, there you go again. Didn't you hear it was one of your fans؟ How is one of your fans going to confuse you for someone else؟"

The thin man had me cornered and was expecting me to take the first wrong step.

"Look, Commander Ramírez," I said, trying to remain respectful, "I really don't know what you're talking about. I was home all evening. Call my parents, they'll tell you."

He arched his eyebrows and rubbed his forehead.

"It's possible, it's possible," he said, "but it's also very possible that you're the Indiana Jones I've been looking for."

"I'm not . . ."

He raised his index finger to shut me up.

"I propose the following: I'm going to go home and sleep for a couple of hours, because I'm really tired . . ."

He grabbed the manila folder, shook it in front of me, and put it on the table.

"I'm going to leave you these documents. Read them calmly and when I come back later, you tell me what you think. Sound good?"

"What are they about?"

"Just legal formalities. You read them and we'll talk later. If you don't agree with anything, we'll discuss it and change the text. Easy, right?"

"And if I do agree?"

My question surprised him. He thought about his answer, took out a fountain pen—a very expensive one—and pointed at a blank space on the backside of one of the pages.

"Real simple: You sign here."

"What with?"

The commander smiled. He held out his arm and gave me the pen.

"With this," he said, "but you take care of it, because my wife gave it to me for Christmas."

He slapped his thighs and stood up.

"We agree then, right?"

He looked at his watch, fixed his jacket, and said good-bye.

"I'll be back before eleven," he assured and turned around to go.

I got up hurriedly and followed him. Upon feeling my presence behind him, he spun around abruptly and faced me.

"What do you want," he asked.

"I want to ask you for two favors."

He relaxed and smiled.

"The first?"

"I haven't eaten all day, could I have something for dinner?"

"Yes, I already had someone go get you some hamburgers."

"Thank you."

"And the second?"

"I absolutely have to pee; please let me go to the bathroom."

"Don't worry, I'll send someone over in five minutes to escort you to the bathroom."

"But please don't let him take too long, because I really can't hold it in any more."

"Sure," he said patting me on the back.

He left and locked the door to the cubicle. Through the blinds I could see him hand the key over to one of my guards. Then I saw him walk away down the hall.

TWENTY, THIRTY MINUTES went by and nobody came to take me to the bathroom. I desperately knocked on the glass door. The two men ignored me.

Frustrated, I had no choice but to pee out the window. I leaned half my body out and, holding on to the window frame, I aimed at the ledge, trying not to sprinkle below me: I didn't want any of the officers waiting around on the pavement to come up and beat the shit out of me. Luckily, the urine flowed across the ledge and formed a stream that discreetly coursed down the wall.

DINNER DIDN'T ARRIVE EITHER, and the rules started to become clear. I depended on the thin man and I had better cooperate with him. For now, my problems boiled down to being unable to urinate in the right place and being a little bit hungry. But he just had to whisper one order to drastically change my situation: beatings, torture, threats, blackmail. To leave me alone in the cubicle was a show of his willingness to negotiate with me. He could've forced me to admit my guilt, but it was better if I admitted freely, without any more trouble to either of us.

WITHIN THE FOLDER were two documents. The first was a confession to several crimes committed, including some I'd never heard of. It was written in the language typical of legal documents and riddled with spelling mistakes.

The second was a declaration by the witness who was incriminating me. It was a pretty accurate narrative of what happened at the zoo, it described me exactly (it even mentioned the gridlike pattern of scars on my left bicep) and it provided the information necessary to find me: my full name, address, telephone number, and the location of the Villalba Motel with the room number I was in. The declaration had been taken that day, at 1:13 PM at a precinct of the Judicial Police of Mexico City. It was signed by Tania Ramos García and under it was a copy of her fingerprint.

It wasn't made up. Tania's signature was authentic. The same one with which she signed so many love letters. The same uneven marks slanting to the right. The same Tania.

The copy of her thumbprint reproduced the slight scar she got on her right thumb when she sliced herself with a box cutter as she was cutting some papers. It was a night when Tania was hurriedly designing a brochure for a school project. The blood gushed abundant and soiled the illustrations she had worked on for hours. She cried in despair: she wouldn't have enough time to do them over. She angrily started to rub her bloodied finger on the other sheets as well. I managed to stop her after she'd made a complete mess. I squeezed the base of her thumb to stop the bleeding, disinfected the wound with hydrogen peroxide, and wrapped her thumb in gauze. Tania kissed me and apologized—she'd gotten blood on me as well.

I REREAD HER TESTIMONY over and over. Her indictment was ruthless. The narrative of facts was cold; my description, detailed, precise, as if she wanted to make sure the police wouldn't err in finding me. She hadn't left any loose ends. There was no evidence of hesitation, no contradictions, no compassionate adjectives. She had been harsh from start to finish.

I grabbed the document that declared I was guilty and, without giving it much thought, signed it. So as not to later regret it, I put it in the folder and slid it under the door. One of the men bent over to pick it up, perused it, and took it to one of the neighboring offices.

I turned out the light and went to huddle against a wall. The smell of Tania's urine still hadn't disappeared from my belly—powerful, long-lasting, painful. I cried for her, and I cried for Gregorio and myself, and for everything we stopped being. I cried for the scar on her thumb that sealed the indictment, and for her betrayal, and for her absence. I cried for what we had lost and what we would lose, for what we were and ceased to be.

I SLEPT FOR A WHILE on the carpet. I was awoken by the silence. I looked through the blinds. None of my guards were there anymore. It wasn't necessary: I'd signed my own sentence, why take care of me?

I opened the window. The air was warm, the night dark. I sat on the windowsill and stayed there till dawn. I saw the cops arrive in their suits, the secretaries, the newspaper boys, the bootblack. I saw secondary school students walk to school, builders eating tacos for breakfast, bureaucrats descending from public transportation.

I heard movement in the office. Secretaries greeting one another, telephones ringing, the opening and closing of filing cabinets, judicial policemen laughing. I heard planes plowing through the sky, the garbage truck's bell, shop owners lifting the metal curtains from their shops.

Jail was imminent. Maybe the sentence would be reduced since I'd voluntarily signed my declaration of guilt, but I didn't expect less than five years of lockup. I ruled out bail: The jaguar's death had angered so many different groups that imprisonment seemed inevitable, as inevitable as the psychiatric ward for Gregorio.

THE COMMANDER came in at ten. Again, he was dressed impeccably. He smelled like lavender and menthol cigarettes. He came into the cubicle, greeted me affably and sat at the table.

"Let me congratulate you," he said.

"Why?"

"For your commitment to the truth," he said snobbishly.

I shrugged my shoulders—what the fuck did he care about the truth?—and I looked out the window again. A stray dog, a puppy, was trying to cross the street unsuccessfully. After gauging several cars, he made his decision and bolted to the other side of the street. He was about to be run over by a truck but it swerved around him at the last minute.

"Lucky, huh?"

I hadn't realized he'd stood up and was watching the same scene I was while he smoked.

"I'm not used to it," he said.

"To what?"

"To people confessing so quickly. It usually takes me at least three or four days."

He gave his cigarette a long drag, blew the smoke out of his nose and continued:

"Why did you sign?"

"Why keep lying?" I answered.

"Either you've got a lot of balls, or you don't know the mess you're getting into."

"Neither," I said.

He gave his cigarette another drag and flicked it into the street. The butt traced an arc and landed on the roof of one of the white Spirits.

"I like you," he said.

I took his pen out of my pants pocket and gave it back to him.

"Thanks," I said.

He took it and put it inside his blazer. As he did, he revealed a glimpse of the butt of a pistol.

"Your parents have been notified. They're coming to see you at twelve."

"Okay."

"They'll bring you some breakfast soon," he pointed out.

He walked out of the cubicle, grabbed a phone from off a desk, and put it on the table.

"Word is bond. You can make as many phone calls as you goddamn well please. Just dial zero to get a dial tone."

"Thanks."

The commander stood there in front of me, smiling.

"You're a present from heaven."

"Why?"

"You made a lot of noise with the tiger thing, and for having arrested you, I'm going to get a promotion, or at least a raise."

"A raise? That's not fair, you had the case solved for you," I said smiling.

The thin man made a face, as if he were surprised by my observation.

"You're right: I had the case solved for me."

We both smiled and he walked over to me.

"Give me your hand and open it," he requested, "I want to show you a magic trick."

He grabbed my middle finger, smiled again and with a sudden movement, bent it all the way backward. I felt a sharp pain radiate all the way to my forearm. Unbearable pain. He let go of me and squeezed my neck affectionately.

"I like you, Manuel, but don't be a smart-ass."

He left the room and locked me in again.

THE PAIN WAS INTENSE. The joint soon became swollen and a purple semi-circle appeared around my knuckle. A cop came in with breakfast on a tray. He put it on the table. There was some ice on a plate. He grabbed three cubes, wrapped them in a handkerchief and gave them to me.

"The commander sent them for your hand," he said and withdrew.

I put the ice on the swelling and the pain slowly diminished. I bandaged my finger in the damp cloth to immobilize it and sat down to have breakfast. They'd brought me a couple of eggs scrambled with ham and onion, an apple and a glass of milk. Other than the onion, I finished everything quickly and was still hungry. The thin man must've guessed as much, because five minutes later another cop came in with three pieces of sweet baked goods and an orange-flavored Jarritos.

When I was done eating I called Tania's house. Laura answered. She told me Tania hadn't slept at home the previous night either, and they didn't now where to find her.

"As you can imagine," she said, "my parents are going insane."

"So am I," I declared.

"Where are you?" she asked.

"In jail," I answered.

"I asked you where you are, not where you deserve to be."

"I told you, in jail. Why?"

"Because I called your house last night and the night before, and your father told me you hadn't been home either."

"And why did you call me?"

"You know my mother, she wanted to know if you'd seen Tania."

"No, I haven't."

"I don't believe you."

"Don't believe me."

"What's going on with you two?"

I was annoyed by the tone in which she asked the question and I just hung up. The pain throbbed again. I removed the cloth. The purple circle had expanded onto the back of my hand. I couldn't bend my finger.

I dialed Jacinto Anaya's number. The stupid machine answered. "Fuck you," I whispered into the receiver and hung up.

A cop came in to pick up the tray. I asked him to take me to the bathroom. He led me through rows of desks, before secretaries who looked at me curiously and judicial policemen who reluctantly got out of the way.

I went into the toilets and the guy waited for me outside. Nobody else was inside and I peed pleasantly, leaning my forehead against the wall. I'd soon lose these little daily intimacies, once I was in jail. This was my main worry: the communal showers and toilets, the cells shared with strangers, cavity searches, supervised visits. Jail would not only remove me from the world, it would remove me from myself, my manias, my habits.

I took off my shirt and looked at myself in the mirror. I'd gotten skinnier. I could see it in my cheeks, my forearms. I turned on the hot water and plugged the basin with toilet paper. I put in my injured hand. Just contact with the water led to penetrating pain. I bore it and left the hand submerged until I could feel the tendons and ligaments relax. I felt some relief, but as soon as I moved my hand it hurt again.

I cleaned my belly of Tania's urine. Then I washed my left arm, my chest and armpits. The cop came in and asked me what was taking so long. To speed things up, I leaned over the sink and washed myself directly under the faucet, bending sideways so the water would cover my torso. I rubbed my face and wet my hair.

I walked out of the bathroom, without drying myself, still dripping, my shirt and pants soaked. Upon seeing me, my custodian made a gesture of disapproval and led me back into the cubicle.

MY PARENTS ARRIVED punctually at twelve. The commander accompanied them to the cubicle and ordered three more chairs to be brought in. They sat before me and the thin man briefly explained my legal situation: a judge had ordered a warrant of arrest for me based on Tania's testimony, and, given the public importance of my case, and the district attorney's concern for resolving it, they had decided to keep me at the precinct before sending me to court. "We will not proceed unless we have all the evidence in hand," he argued. My father asked if the decision to keep me in custody was illegal. The thin man emphasized that my rights had been respected and that I had been given special treatment since I was "from a good family." My father stroked his mustache as he listened; my mother had tears in her eyes. "The young man has fully accepted responsibility for his actions," he concluded, "and must maturely undergo whatever punishment is imposed on him." Upon hearing my mother cry, he turned to her.

"He's not a boy anymore, ma'am," he said.

My mother lowered her head and pressed against the edges of her eyes to stop crying.

"I'll retire so you can speak alone," he said with propriety.

We remained silent for a few minutes. My father looked overwhelmed, as if the situation exceeded his physical and emotional capabilities. His lower lip was trembling slightly. His gaze slipped over objects and he constantly swallowed saliva. My mother, despite her sobbing, didn't seem afflicted. It was evident that she could barely hold in her anger.

My father started to speak in a broken voice. He told me he couldn't understand why I had done it, but that they were with me and were going to work to free me as soon as possible. They had tried to contact Mr. Derbez, the ex–minister of finance who had been my mother's boss, but they had been unable to find him. To defend me, they had hired a prestigious criminal lawyer, the friend of a cousin of my mother's.

"I know a very good lawyer who gets people out of jail for a living. He may be better than yours," I said, thinking about Tania's father's partner.

"What do you know about lawyers?" my mother scolded.

"It was just a suggestion," I argued.

"We're not interested in your suggestions," she pointed out.

"We trust this lawyer," my father intervened, trying to conciliate.

"Have it your way," I said.

"Of course we're going to have it our way," bellowed my mother.

"Whatever," I said.

My mother looked at me, furious.

"Are you making fun of me?"

"No."

"You better not be."

I shut up to avoid provoking her any more. But my mother had already become enraged and it was difficult to stop her.

"Why did you do this to us?" she asked.

"I didn't do anything to you."

"Oh no?"

"No."

"You did it to get at us."

"You're paranoid delusional, Mom."

"You've always been so impertinent," she said.

The word *impertinent* irritated me. It seemed like a qualifier stupid, snooty ladies used to talk down to their servants.

"The apple doesn't fall far from the tree," I said.

My mother got up and tried to slap me, but I blocked her with my forearm.

"You're ruining our lives," she screamed.

My father got between us and hugged my mother.

"Calm down, Malena, don't make things more difficult."

My mother pushed him away to free herself. She turned

around, walked out and slammed the door. The glass shook as if it were about to detach.

"It's not fair that you behave like that with her," my father exclaimed.

"I'm sorry," I whispered.

"Your mother and I are very tense; we never thought we'd be in circumstances like this."

"Neither did I."

"If you'd only tell us what was going on."

"Nothing, nothing's going on."

"This is because of Gregorio, isn't it?"

"No."

He sat back down and crossed his arms.

"Is it true that you were arrested in a motel?"

"Yes."

"What were you doing there?"

"I rent a room there."

My father appeared amazed.

"What for?"

"Tania and I rented it so we could be alone."

"For how long?"

"About two years."

He inhaled deeply and whistled as he exhaled.

"Now I understand," he said with the face of one putting two and two together. But no, my father would never be able to understand.

There was a silence uncomfortable for both of us.

"How's Luis?" I asked.

"Fine."

"Does he know where I am?"

My father nodded. I was sorry that my brother knew. How

would he explain what I'd done to his uninteresting friends and girlfriends?

"Do you want me to look for the lawyer you mentioned?" he asked.

"If you can."

"Who is he?"

"One of the partners from Tania's father's law firm."

"Tania's father?" he asked. "After what she did to you?"

I shrugged my shoulders.

"They say he's very good. Besides, he knows me and I think he likes me."

"What's his name?"

"I don't know his name, but everybody knows him as 'Tuercas' Manrique."

"I'll look for him."

My father got up, walked toward me, and grabbed my shoulders.

"We're going to get you out of this," he assured me.

"It doesn't matter."

"What?"

"If you don't get me out, honestly, it doesn't matter."

He took a step back and looked at me.

"Sometimes I don't know who you are anymore, son," he mumbled and left.

AN HOUR LATER, the lawyer my parents had hired arrived. He was tall and in his fifties, with blue eyes and freckles on his bald pate. He stank of the same lavender lotion the thin man used. "I'm Attorney Olvera," he introduced himself. He handed me his card and succinctly expounded his strategy for my defense: a psychiatrist friend of his would evaluate me and between the both of them they would attenuate the report in order to prove that I was suffering from a transitory mental disturbance provoked by my best friend's suicide. "We're going to find extenuating circumstances to keep you locked up for as little as possible, even if we have to argue that you're a little crazy," he concluded with a smile. He excused himself with a handshake and left. I tore his card up into little pieces and threw them out the window.

AT THREE I ATE a couple of Cuban sandwiches sent to me by the commander (full of onion, for a change) and they let me go to the bathroom again. When I came back, I could see someone talking with my parents farther off. It was almost certainly the psychiatrist recommended by Olvera. He put on the gestures common to everyone in his profession: he tilted his head when he spoke, he stroked his chin, gazed condescendingly, and didn't stop moving his head, like a bobblehead doll in a taxi. Worst of all, he looked almost exactly like Doctor Macías, only a little fatter.

I walked into the cubicle, lay down on the carpet, and fell asleep. I dreamt of Gregorio and Tania. The three of us were dressed in our secondary school uniforms and we were walking down a long, endless street. As we walked the pavement turned into softer matter. Walking became difficult and our shoes were getting stuck in the asphalt mud. Suddenly, the floor gave way under us and we plunged in up to our waists. The three of us were holding out our hands, trying to get out of the enveloping pulp. They were drowning as I slowly sank.

The thin man woke me up, shaking me by the shoulder. I opened my eyes and for a few seconds I couldn't figure out where I was. The thin man held out his hand and helped me up. "You sleep heavy," he said. "I've been trying to wake you up for five minutes." He walked over to the table, grabbed a plastic bag, and held it up.

Inside was the gun with which I'd shot the jaguar. I was surprised that the thin man's detectives had found it. They must have gone from sewer to sewer looking for it. He showed it to me.

"That's the one you shot the tiger with, right?"

"Jaguar," I corrected.

"It's the same thing, man."

"Yeah, that's the one."

The commander opened the door and called one of his subordinates, who came in and put several black ink pads and a few white cards on the table.

"We're going to take your fingerprints," he said.

He took each and every one of my fingerprints. He even made me use my injured finger. No sooner had I touched it against the piece of card then lacerating pain made me pull it away brusquely. The ink smudged on the card leaving an amorphous stain. The man looked displeased, but the commander ordered him with a look to continue the procedure.

Once I finished, he handed me a cloth and some alcohol to clean my hands.

"That's it," the man said and left.

The commander took the cards and arranged them like a poker hand.

"We're going to compare these prints with the ones on the gun to see if they match."

"They'll match," I affirmed.

"Goddammit, let me do my job, will you?"

We both smiled. He pulled out a piece of paper from his pocket and read it to himself. He folded it again and put it away.

"The gun is registered under the name Arnulfo Camariña Iglesias. Do you know him?"

"Yeah, he's the owner of the motel where you arrested me."

"What were you doing with his gun?"

"I stole it."

"What for?"

"To hunt jaguars."

He laughed out loud.

"You're too much."

He told me that later I'd be taken to sleep in an office with its own bathroom. I thanked him.

"District attorney's orders," he clarified, "not mine."

My mother's ties to high-level politicians had started to have an effect. Even if I didn't avoid jail, at least I'd enjoy some privileges.

I WASN'T WRONG. The guy I'd seen with my parents had, in fact, been the psychiatrist proposed by Olvera. He turned out to be more pleasant than I'd thought. He joked with me about my cell/cubicle and about my twisted finger: "That's what you get for making gestures at cops."

Without being pedantic, he asked me several questions: "Have you felt depressed lately?" "Did you ever commit another crime?" "Do you have a police record?" "Any trouble with your parents?" "Problems with your girlfriend?" "Fear of death?"

At first I answered confidently, even occasionally joking, but I don't know how or why, I started to waver, to contradict myself, to reveal fears not even I had imagined, to lose control. I blurted out confused phrases with a dizzying lack of coherence, until I cracked. At that moment, I understood the full force of Macías's sentence: Madness can be more terrifying than death.

The fat man, whose name I didn't know then, nor do I now, got up from his chair and did what I thought psychiatrists never did: He hugged me. Not an impersonal hug, but a deep, affectionate one. I wanted to tell him about the night buffalo, about its breath on my neck, its gallop on the plains of death, about Gregorio and the earwigs that devoured him, about the evening we cut each other with knives, about how much I hated onions, about Tania's betrayal, her love, and how my sadness at her absence was killing me, about how much it meant to me to be able to pee on my own, about Rebecca's torso, Margarita's imperfect body, about my friend René being decapitated in a car accident, about the time, as a kid, that I cut my brother with a scalpel. Sunk in a paralyzing stupor, I was unable to say a word.

The fat man waited for me to calm down and I gradually recovered control of myself. I felt exhausted—my muscles flaccid, out of breath, as if I'd just made an extraordinary physical effort. The fat man squatted next to me.

"Are you feeling better?"

I nodded and the fat man went to sit on the other chair.

"What's your favorite food?" he asked.

His question seemed absurd, out of place.

"Grilled ham and cheese sandwiches," I answered.

"That's it?"

"Also sweet and sour chicken, garlic shrimp, and pepper steak."

"You've got gourmet tastes, and expensive gourmet tastes at that!"

He thought about my answers for a moment and lightly hit his chin with his fist.

"Do you know what they feed you in jail?" he asked.

"No," I answered annoyed.

"Beans, a piece of bread, fried eggs drenched in oil, coffee, sometimes meatballs or pork and greens. Do you know how I know?"

I shook my head.

"Because I was in jail for three years, eight months, fourteen days, and nine hours."

It didn't look like he was lying, trying to console me, or even trying to win my sympathy.

"It was fucking awful, and when I got out of there I promised I'd never let what happened to me happen to others."

He looked at my hand and pointed at my hurt finger.

"For example: I don't want another fucking cop to bend your finger backward, and you know what I'm talking about, right?"

He raised his left hand and showed me two crooked fingers.

WE TALKED FOR A LONG TIME. I never trusted anyone as much as I did him. He asked me to listen to his instructions, to fake it if I had to, and not to sign another document without talking to him first. He hugged me good-bye.

Like many people I crossed paths with in my life, I never saw him again.

AT NIGHTFALL, "Tuercas" Manrique arrived. I didn't want to see anyone else. The session with the psychiatrist had left me exhausted. He found me splayed out on the carpet, sleeping. I got up lethargically and said hello. Manrique was a restless, witty man, but this time I noticed he was reserved.

"I appreciate you thinking of me for your case," he said, "but I don't think I'll be of much use to you."

He seemed worried: I'd admitted my guilt and he would have trouble arguing that I had been coerced. He explained that the list of charges was long and the serious accusations not only centered on the jaguar, but on my having attacked Tania with a loaded weapon.

"But I didn't try to attack her," I clarified, indignant, "that's ridiculous."

"I know, but Tania went all out against you."

He was considering four ways of defending me: The first was to force Tania to ratify her declaration. The second was to set up a face-to-face meeting between us. The third was to deny the charges and claim that psychological pressure and threats were used to get my confession. And the fourth was to claim that I was emotionally disturbed. The last one seemed the most viable. He had already consulted with Olvera and the psychiatrist, and between the three of them they had agreed to prepare a joint defense.

I was opposed to all of the alternatives. The first two meant confronting Tania, and I didn't have the courage to do so. Besides, I couldn't forget that "Tuercas," as Tania's father's partner, would not get involved in the process. The other two meant lying, and I wanted to find my ground again.

"Have it your way," said "Tuercas," disappointed.

He pointed out that luckily my name was no longer in the headlines, though it wouldn't be long before Commander Ramírez leaked it to some reporter in order to secure his raise. Also, Manrique had already talked to the district attorney about my case ("With my bestest buddy," he joked) and he had assured him that he would under no circumstances bargain for my freedom, neither would he bend to the desires of retired public officials, clearly referring to the ex–minister of finance—my mother's old boss. "He's a man I respect," he'd said, "but now he's spent ammunition, and he doesn't have the slightest political power to pressure me." He did, however, promise that I'd be given the best possible treatment while I was under his jurisdiction.

"And since you don't want to help us or yourself," Manrique concluded, "you're going to have no choice but to give up and go to the slammer."

I wasn't giving up. I just considered all my ways out to be cut off. The cost of avoiding prison seemed higher than the cost of accepting it.

Manrique must have left that cubicle convinced that I really did suffer from some sort of emotional infirmity.

AT EIGHT O'CLOCK, two cops arrived to transfer me. We walked down dozens of hallways through forgotten desks and boxes of files piled on top of one another. We arrived at a spacious and comfortable office with a large window that looked out onto an avenue. A dark wood table and a black leather couch took up half the space. There were several phone jacks, but no phones. They had put a sleeping bag and my pillow in a corner—the same pillow I had used since I was a boy. It was a pillow thick with its feather stuffing, and a rayon pillowcase. Also, my blue flannel pajamas. Instead of comforting me, the familiar objects made me feel attacked. They were home intruding in the chaos of my collapse, the painful reminder of a world to which I neither could nor wanted to return. I put my pajamas in the pillow and threw them into a filing cabinet.

AS THE THIN MAN had promised, the room had its own bathroom. I sat on the toilet lid with the lights off. A constant murmur indicated that one of the pipes had cracked and the water was spilling into the drainage. The walls smelled like humidity. Who invented bathrooms and when did he do it? Who invented toilets, showers, and washbasins? Whose idea was it to mix hot and cold water, who thought of toothbrushes, soap, razor blades, combs? I considered bathrooms to be the saddest places in the world, and I, in the bathroom of that office, felt sadder than ever.

ONE AFTERNOON in the motel, after making love, Tania told me the story of an eighty-seven-year-old man who was in an intensive care unit due to a stroke. He was a Frenchman who had settled down in Mexico at the age of twenty, recently married to a woman named Marie. He was a man dedicated to his work and family. He was meticulous. Two days after he had been checked into the hospital, he began to speak in the patois of his native region, which he hadn't spoken in over sixty years, not even with his wife, since she was from another province.

At his most critical moments, the old man would incessantly say the name Valerie, and ask anyone who visited him about her. His wife, when she heard this, refused to ever see him again and muttered between her teeth, "Let him rot." The sons and grandchildren wondered what was behind this name to cause such marital stress. Two months later, Marie died and the old man went on with his senile delusions. He gradually stopped recognizing those around him: his sons, their wives, his friends. He only repeated the monotonous "Valerie." No one in the family could unravel the mystery until one of the old man's cousins arrived from France. Valerie was the name of the girlfriend his parents had forced him to break up with in order to marry Marie. The old man had to abandon Valerie with a sense of defeat that lasted sixty-seven years. He never saw or heard anything about her again. He only once went back to France—to Paris—to deal with some legal matters regarding an inheritance.

I imagined the man in the hospital room groping the breasts of a fifteen-year-old girl in empty space, kissing her neck, whispering how much he loved her in his patois, yearning for her until his final breath.

Tania finished telling me the story and fell asleep on my chest. At the time I thought she had told me this story to let me know I was the man of her life. Now, it pains me to admit it, I think she meant Gregorio.

THE SILENCE INSIDE the office was total. They say one of the worst things about prison is the lack of silence. There is always a shout, a voice, a drop of water, steps, snoring. I had to make the most of it; this was probably my last night of silence.

I SLEPT DEEPLY. My exhaustion was such that I hadn't realized I'd rested my face on a thumbtack. In the middle of the early morning, the thin man walked in with three cops. He turned on the light and woke me by pushing me with the sole of his shoe.

I sat up and rubbed my eyes. I was suddenly invaded by the fear of being tortured. I asked what was going on.

"You're outta here," the commander answered.

I supposed I was going to be transferred to isolation or maybe even to jail.

"Where to?" I asked nervously.

The commander smiled with a harsh, tight expression.

"Home, buddy."

"Why?"

The commander squatted before me.

"I don't have the slightest fucking idea who you are, but you've got some pretty powerful friends backing you, that's for sure."

"What are you talking about?"

"The minister of the interior asked the D.A., or should I say ordered him, to let you go. How d'you like that?"

I didn't know what to say.

"The boss is pretty fucking pissed off," he continued, "but he has no choice but to comply, so get the hell up and get the hell out before somebody upstairs regrets it."

I got out of the sleeping bag and sat down to put my shoes on. The commander handed me two folders.

"They're yours," he said.

They were the original copies of Tania's and my declaration.

"Keep them as a souvenir, tear 'em up, or stick 'em up your ass," he joked.

He looked bothered. He didn't seem to find my release funny at all. I got up. The thin man brushed off some carpet fuzz from my shirt and pointed at my cheek.

"You're bleeding," he warned.

The thumbtack had punctured me, but I felt no pain.

"Let's go," he ordered.

We walked down the hallways in the darkness. We arrived at a desk near the cubicle I had been kept in before. The commander opened a drawer and he took out the gun Camariña had given me, wrapped in a plastic bag.

"I'm giving it back to you," he said.

He took out some sheets and started to tear them into pieces.

"They're copies of your confession and your girlfriend's accusation."

He also tore up the cards with my fingerprints.

"These are the orders from the D.A.," he clarified. "You were never here, you understand? Never . . ."

He grew quiet and looked at my injured finger.

"And of course, I didn't do that to you, did I?"

I shook my head. We walked to the elevators escorted by the cops, who looked underslept and grumpy. We got into the elevator and one of them pushed the button for the lobby.

The doors opened. There were several other cops on guard in the lobby. Some of them looked mistrustfully at the bagged weapon I was carrying in my hand. The thin man signaled one of his subordinates to open the main door. Then he grabbed me by the shoulder and pushed me toward the street.

"Leave now," he said.

I walked down the steps. A patrol car with its turret lit screeched past and drove down to the underground parking lots. I asked one of the judicial policemen walking around there what time it was. "Four-twenty," he answered.

I sat on the sidewalk without knowing what to do. I didn't have a single peso and I didn't even know where I was supposed to go.

I went back to the building to look for the commander. A

judicial cop stopped me at the entrance. "Where are you going?" he asked brusquely. I pointed at the commander, who was still in the lobby. "To talk to him," I answered.

The judicial cop let him know and the thin man came to see me.

"You miss me, don't you," he said without smiling.

I explained that I had no way to get home.

"I don't give a shit."

"You can't just leave me stranded like this," I protested.

"I just did," he mocked.

He spun around and walked back into the building. I followed and cut in front of him.

"At least give me a ride."

He looked me up and down and kept walking. Again, I got in his way.

"Ooh!" he exclaimed, "it hasn't been two minutes since I let you go and you already think you're a tough guy."

"It's four-thirty in the morning and I can't get home," I insisted.

He looked at his watch and shook his head.

"You're wrong: it's four twenty-five . . ."

"It's just that . . ." I began to protest when he turned around and gripped my left ring finger.

"'It's just that' my ass," he said and started to bend it backward. I tried to break loose but he tightened his grip with his other hand.

"I can break each and every one of your fingers if you don't get the fuck out of here," he warned.

He let go of me and several cops surrounded me threateningly.

"Get out," he said, snapping his fingers.

I walked toward the door. Before I left the thin man called out to me.

"Besides, quit whining," he said, "we've already told your lawyer; he'll be here any minute."

I sat on the steps to wait for him. So as not to look suspicious, I hid the gun in my shirt. At first the cops kept looking at me, but eventually they forgot about me.

MANRIQUE ARRIVED at seven in the morning.

"God, you're lucky," he said when he saw me.

He grabbed me by the arm and helped me up. He looked a lot less tense than the previous day.

"This has been the easiest case of my life," he joked.

He bought me a glass of orange juice in a nearby street stall. He explained that the minister of the interior's orders had been direct, and that the district attorney had had no choice but to follow them immediately.

"I thought you said he didn't take orders from anyone . . ." I mocked him.

"Yeah, well, where there's a captain . . . sailors obey."

I asked if the minister of the interior had acted because of my mother's influence. "That didn't do any good," he said, laughing as he gave his juice a sip. He explained that the person who had interceded for me had been the minister's stepson: Jacinto Anaya.

"Who?" I asked, awestruck.

"Jacinto Anaya," Manrique repeated, smiling.

I couldn't believe it.

"Why?"

Manrique looked at me, estranged.

"What? Isn't he your friend?"

I shook my head.

"Well, he must be," he concluded, "because he helped you out a bunch."

I felt defenseless. It seemed as if Jacinto had effected my release to have me all to himself. Again, Gregorio's distant will was intervening in my destiny. When would he leave me alone? When?

"You don't look very happy," said Manrique. He patted me on the thigh and paid for the juices. "Let's go, I'll take you home."

We got into the car. It wasn't even eight and already you could feel the suffocating heat. Manrique turned on the air-conditioning and put some classical music in the tape deck.

"So you can relax," he suggested.

He told me my parents hadn't been informed of my liberation yet.

"You're going to surprise them," he affirmed.

I led him to the motel instead of my house. A couple of blocks before we reached it, I pointed at a gray house with a red gate. "That's where I live," I told him. Manrique kept going, drove around the street, and parked in front of the motel.

"Don't forget that I'm your lawyer," he said, "and that lawyers know everything about their clients."

I felt stupid.

"Don't sweat it, man," he said, "just trust me next time."

We agreed he'd inform my parents of my freedom without telling them where I was. He lent me two hundred pesos "as an expense account," he said jokingly, and wrote his home number on one of his business cards.

"Only if it's an emergency," he warned when he gave it to me.

• • •

I WENT INTO THE MOTEL. Pancho saw me from a distance and hurried over to me.

"How are you?" he asked.

"So so," I answered.

"The boss and I were real worried," he said.

He told me that three or four times, the judicial police had been there to interrogate them about who I was, what I did, who I went to the motel with, how often, etcetera. He said they'd even taken Camariña's fingerprints.

"What'd you do?" he asked curiously.

"They had me confused with someone else," I said.

"I thought so," said Pancho.

I took the gun out from under my shirt and gave it to him.

"Please, give it back to Mr. Camariña," I asked.

I went to the room. I opened the door. It smelled like floor cleaner. Everything looked like it was in order: the bed, the curtains, the mirror, the dressing table. I sat on the mattress. Ruvalcaba's book had disappeared from the nightstand. I felt a great emptiness, as if the last of my ties to Tania had been severed. I walked out and asked Pancho if she'd come.

"She slept here two nights ago," he said, "and left yesterday afternoon."

I went back to the room. As I got naked to have a shower, I discovered a piece of LifeSaver wrapping on the edge of the dressing table. I picked it up, folded it carefully and put it in my wallet.

I finished my shower, lay on the bed, and went to sleep.

• • •

I LOCKED MYSELF in the room for several days. I didn't want to leave it or talk to anybody. I slept for most of the time. Sometimes I was awakened by a sharp throbbing in my finger that made me run to the bathroom to put my hand under hot water. The piercing pain would diminish after a long time and the five or six aspirins I swallowed in one gulp.

I was also awakened by the buffalo's huffing. I would jump out of bed and breathe until I could calm down. Once I was terrified: The huffing went on throughout an entire day. I could hear the breath vibrate around the room: incessant, furious. I was closer to madness than ever.

I missed Tania much more than I thought I would and I'm sure she needed me even more. She must have been losing her mind like me, fighting to elude her guilt, her fears, her lies. And I missed her more every minute.

I knew Jacinto Anaya was after me, and that through him, Gregorio would continue to stalk me. Jacinto had acted much more intelligently than I had. He wasn't the simpleton I'd imagined by a long shot. His plays were elegant, unexpected, and it was hard to intuit what he would do next.

I SOON RAN OUT OF MONEY. I spent the two hundred pesos Manrique had lent me ordering pizzas with salami to the room. After handing them over, the delivery boys would stand there expecting a tip, but I would close the door without saying a word.

I had to borrow money from Pancho. He barely managed fifty pesos. I used half of it to buy a box of Dolac at the corner drugstore (aspirin wasn't working anymore), and I wasted the rest of it on food. Fifteen minutes later I found myself without money to eat again.

Camariña sent me *Reforma* and *Excelsior* every morning.

Maybe he guessed that I really had gotten myself into trouble and supposed that I wanted to find out about something. Or maybe he just sent them so I had something to read, so I wouldn't get so bored. At first the newspapers followed up on the incident at the zoo and even mentioned that the police were after two or three suspects. They ran the sketch of Gregorio again, and they asked their readers to help find him. In an interview, the district attorney assured he wouldn't rest until they'd found the person "responsible for such an atrocious deed." He had the balls to promise a maximum of a month before they found the culprit.

A week later, the newspapers had almost entirely forgotten about the affair when one night a homeless man killed himself by jumping onto the subway tracks. Despite being unrecognizable, the police soon identified him as the criminal and closed the case. A few days later, the press communicated that commander Martín Ramírez had been given a promotion for having solved such a "delicate investigation." I imagined the thin man with his courteous, feminine gestures, toasting to my health.

I'D ASKED PANCHO AND CAMARIÑA to tell anyone who came looking for me that I wasn't there. The first three days there was nobody, but on the fourth my parents had come. According to Pancho, they looked very worried. They knew I was free but had no idea where to find me (they couldn't find Tania either). Pancho assured them he hadn't seen me around the motel. They became even more distressed and left upset. Pancho confessed to me that he regretted lying to them. "I really felt sorry for them, Manuel," he said.

That night I called them to ease their minds. My mother apologized to me, and I to her. "I love you very, very much," she said, crying. She sounded really scared. I explained that I hadn't come home because I needed to think things over, that it wasn't their fault that I'd stayed away and that I'd soon return. She sent me a kiss and we hung up. My mother.

I also called "Tuercas" Manrique. When he heard my voice, he greeted me jokingly. He had found it amusing that they should blame the homeless suicide for the shootings at the zoo.

"He must've looked like you," he joked.

I asked him if he could lend me some money.

"As an expense account," I clarified.

"No," he answered bluntly, "I've done my job as a lawyer. Now you have to scratch yourself with your own nails."

The bastard said good-bye laughing his ass off.

CAMARIÑA, who had heard my conversation with Manrique from his office, came over to me and gave me four hundred pesos, and didn't allow me to refuse them.

"You can pay me some other time," he said.

He noticed my injured hand. He looked at it and told me that he had once also dislocated a finger trying to catch a mule that had gone wild. He took out a first-aid kit, rubbed tiger balm on my finger, and put a splint on it.

"Keep it on for three weeks," he said.

Thanks to him, for the first night in a long time I slept a painless sleep.

THE NEXT MORNING, Pancho woke me up.

"This came for you," he said and showed me a letter. I immediately recognized Jacinto Anaya's handwriting on it.

I took it and tore it up without opening it. Pancho looked at me perplexed.

"Why are you tearing it up?"

"Because I know what it says."

"And what does it say?"

"Nothing important," I answered.

I asked him who'd brought it.

"I don't know," he answered, "somebody left it on the reception desk in the early morning."

The next day another letter arrived, which I also tore up. Like the last one, it had been left at the reception desk when no one was there.

That night I dialed Jacinto's number. Neither he nor the machine answered. I tried several times: nothing. I was frustrated not to find him. Now Jacinto could be anywhere, out of my reach. I didn't even have the consolation of cursing at his answering machine anymore.

TWO DAYS LATER, Pancho gave me a transparent plastic bag, sealed with tape. It had a piece of paper on it that said: "For Manuel Aguilera, room 803, a souvenir." It was written in a script I didn't recognize. A strange hand, clearly female, whose letters were too bunched up and whose "e"s and "l"s were the same size. Who the hell was joining the game now? Some friend of Jacinto's? His girlfriend? Or a new messenger from Gregorio acting on his own?

Inside the bag were two Polaroid snapshots of Tania. Behind the pictures Tania had written: "February fourth, once again." She was sitting on a bed in a room I didn't recognize but that looked very much like a motel. Tania was staring languidly, her hair covering part of her face, resting her elbows on her knees. It looked as if she had just spoken a word, with her lips still parted, her eyebrows raised and a half smile.

In the other she was standing on a hill in a park I also couldn't identify (why do the women we love come to know places so foreign to us?). Tania was looking the other way, with her arms crossed, pensive. The photographer's shadow was projected onto the path. It must have been either very late or very early, because the shadow stretched all the way to a nearby bench. It looked like the silhouette of a man. Probably Gregorio's.

I'd already lost Tania, my best friend, my best enemy. I'd lost myself. What did Gregorio gain from rubbing my nose in it? What the hell did he gain?

I put the photographs under my pillow and slept on them.

A FEW DAYS went by and I didn't receive any more letters or photographs. Maybe Gregorio's arsenal had run out. I called my parents on several occasions, but since I could hear they were more and more anxious, I stopped. It pained me that they were starting to sound frightened of me.

I called Tania's friends to ask where she was, but most of them hadn't seen her in two weeks. Only Monica Abín had spoken to her recently. Tania had suddenly shown up at her house to borrow some blouses and skirts. She made up some absurd excuse that Monica didn't want to dwell on. "I'll give them back on Monday," she said. Then she vanished without a trace.

I used the money Camariña had given me as best I could. Instead of spending it all on pizzas, I decided to buy cheap groceries that wouldn't spoil easily: cereals, ultrapasteurized milk, white bread, canned tuna and sardines, a crate of large Cock-Colas, juice, fruit, and for dessert: apple and mango Gerber baby food.

March turned out to be an excessively hot month. It was unbearable to be in the room, but I didn't like to be away from it. I felt protected in the motel and to leave it made me anxious. In the mornings I'd sit in the hallway to watch TV with Camariña. All there was to watch were intensely boring programs that Camariña made entertaining with his sarcastic remarks. He especially made fun of a talk-show host in her forties who was hell-bent on wearing mini-skirts that revealed her varicose veins. "Uh oh!" Camariña exclaimed every time the lady crossed her legs, "the blue worm strikes again!"

At midday, Camariña would lock himself in his office to do the accounting and he'd put the TV away. Then I'd lean on the wall outside my room to watch the couples come in. They almost all went through the same routine: the women would duck or cover themselves and the men would look dead ahead; after parking, they'd get out to pay with false conviction and a look that said "I've done this a thousand times." As soon as the men got out, most of the women would seize the opportunity to spruce themselves up a little in the passenger mirror. There were exceptions: women determined to pay for the room; men who sank into the passenger seat or hid their faces with a newspaper; men who took a long time fixing their hair in the rearview mirror, making sure there was no lipstick on their collar.

At night I'd lie naked on the bed with the light on, bearing the heat, waiting for the buffalo to charge.

• • •

ONE NIGHT, at about eleven, the guy with the curly hair knocked on the door to tell me there was a phone call for me at the reception desk.

"Do you know who it is?" I asked him.

He answered by shrugging his shoulders.

"How are you?" asked Jacinto as soon as I answered.

"Very hot," I answered, immediately recognizing his voice.

"You know who it is, right?"

"Yes."

"That's a drag, isn't it," he said after a pause.

"What?"

"That: the heat," he clarified.

We were both quiet for a few instants.

"What do you want?" I asked.

"We never had a chance to talk."

"You chickened out," I told him.

"I never chicken out," he claimed.

"Well, at the zoo, I'm pretty sure you did."

I gestured to the curly-haired guy that everything was okay and that he could go. He had been standing next to me during the entire conversation.

"You don't understand, man," Jacinto assured me.

"Oh no?"

"No, you don't understand anything."

"Why don't you explain it to me?"

"That's why I'm calling, to explain."

"Over the phone or in person."

"In person."

"When?"

"Now, if you want," he said.

"You don't have the balls."

"Of course I do. If you don't believe me, look behind you."

I turned slowly. Jacinto was staring at me from outside the window in the reception area with a cell phone in his hand.

"As you can see, I have the balls."

I hung up and Jacinto smiled. He made a gesture with his arms asking me to come outside. I walked out of the door in front of him. He was taller, more robust than I'd imagined.

"It was about time we met," he said sardonically.

"What for?"

"To talk of many things."

"Talk."

Jacinto signaled with his chin over at the guy with the curly hair, who was now watching us from five yards away.

"You don't mind if he hears us?" he asked.

"I don't care," I answered.

Jacinto shook his head.

"No, somewhere else," he ordered.

"Okay, let's go to the room."

Jacinto smiled.

"Better . . ."

We got there and I sat on the unmade bed. Jacinto pointed at the stool in front of the dressing table.

"Can I sit down?"

I nodded. Jacinto dropped heavily onto it. It seemed as if the stool had cracked. He adjusted and looked around the room.

"So this is the famous room 803," he said.

His comment irritated me, but before I could protest Jacinto stood up again.

"Can I use your bathroom?"

"Go ahead," I said, holding out my hand.

Jacinto went in and locked the door. I got up, took three

empty glass bottles from the crate of Cock-Colas and hid them in case things got violent: one under the bed, another behind the curtains, and the third under the nightstand.

Jacinto came out buckling his belt and sat on the stool again. He looked at me fixedly, took out a bandanna from his pants pocket and mopped the sweat off his forehead.

"So this is where you met with Tania," he asked.

"Yeah, why?"

"It's pretty shitty, don't you think?"

"Stop fucking with me," I said. "And if you've got something to say to me, stop beating around the goddamn bush and say it."

Without reacting, Jacinto carefully folded his bandanna and put it away again.

"Don't take offense, it was just a thought."

"Like it was just a thought to send me Gregorio's letters, right?"

"Maybe."

"You're a little old to be playing the middleman."

"This isn't a game. Neither Gregorio nor I are playing."

"Gregorio's dead, didn't they tell you?"

He shook his head.

"Stop bullshitting me and tell me what you want," I said.

Jacinto opened his hands and clicked his tongue several times.

"To tell you the truth, I don't want anything."

"Then stop fucking with me."

He looked at me threateningly.

"You don't like people to fuck with you, do you? But you sure do like fucking with other people."

I slid my hand down to where I'd hidden the bottle under the bed.

"Like who?" I asked.

"Gregorio, for one," he answered.

"Gregorio? Gregorio destroyed everything he touched."

"Not me."

"You were lucky."

He suddenly stood up and pointed at a milk carton.

"Do you mind if I have some?" he asked. "I have to take some medication."

I poured him some in a plastic cup. Jacinto took out two pills from a blue box and swallowed them with a big gulp.

"Thanks," he said.

He put the cup on the dressing table, sat down again, and leaned back.

"You've never been locked up in a mental institution, have you?"

"No."

He sighed and looked at the floor as if he were remembering something.

"When you're in there," he continued, turning his eyes toward me, "you're held by very thin strings, and when those strings snap everything becomes a whirlwind. There's no north, no south, no down, no up, no left, no right. You understand?"

"No, I don't understand."

He lifted his hands to his head, pulled his hair back and cleared his throat. His voice sounded deeper.

"Do you know the name of the string that held Gregorio?"

"No."

"Her name was Tania."

I laughed at the provocation.

"Well, it turns out," I added, "that that was the name of my string, too."

"Yes," he said and tapped his temple with his index finger repeatedly, "but you've never gotten lost in here."

"Don't be so sure."

"No, you don't know what that's like. I'm speaking from personal experience. You don't have the slightest fucking idea."

"Yes, I do, it's just that some of us are stronger than others."

Jacinto bit a hangnail off his thumb and shook his head.

"And you say that it was Gregorio who destroyed everything."

"Yeah, so much so," I affirmed, "that he destroyed himself."

"Or maybe he got a little help."

"Look," I told him, "Gregorio was my best friend, I'd known him for a long time and I watched him break apart on his own. There wasn't much you could do, I can assure you."

"You weren't his friend," he shot back angrily, "you wrecked him."

"We both hit each other with everything we had—with everything."

"And who lost?"

"This isn't about who won or who lost."

"Who lost," he insisted.

"Neither of us did, goddammit!"

"He's dead and you're here, taking it easy."

I started waving my hands as I protested.

"He killed himself because he wanted to. What the fuck do I have to do with it?"

"You don't realize, do you?"

"Realize what?"

"That you're the one who destroys everything. Why do you think Tania runs away from you all the time?"

I was tempted to pick up the glass bottle and crack it across his head.

"Don't bring Tania into this again, or I'll make you swallow your own balls."

"Oh, that's scary," he said.

We remained silent, sizing each other up. Jacinto was large, but I was sure I could beat him down with the bottle.

"Tania's the reason I'm here," he said.

"What?"

"She's scared of you, Manuel, very scared."

"Whatever Tania feels or doesn't feel for me, is my problem."

"Well, she's fucking terrified of you."

"Okay, okay, so?"

"Gregorio was afraid of you, too."

I didn't answer back anymore. His words, his gaze, ceased being threatening and turned somber.

"You shouldn't have gone out with Tania," he said.

"Those things happen."

"No, those things are avoided."

"So now you're a moralist?" I told him.

Jacinto remained silent, wrinkling his brow every now and again.

"Tania and I didn't fall in love on purpose," I added, but Jacinto didn't pay attention.

He took out the bandanna again, wiped the sweat off the back of his neck, and started to talk in a low voice.

"Several years ago, in a place in Africa I went to, it was so hot that the lakes started to dry up . . ."

He paused to put the bandanna away and went on.

"They dried up so quickly that all that was left was some spots of filthy water, with thousands of fish belly up and stinking. You can't imagine the smell."

He finished and was quiet.

"And?" I asked.

He gulped and looked me in the eyes.

"That's what you must smell like inside," he answered.

He didn't say another word. He got up and walked toward the door. I got in his way.

"Where's Tania?" I asked.

"I don't know," he answered.

"You know where she went, don't think I'm an idiot."

"I really don't know."

He stepped aside to go on his way, but I intercepted him again.

"You still haven't told me lots of things."

"That's all I had to say to you."

I grabbed the pictures of Tania I'd received the previous week and showed them to him.

"What about these?"

He grabbed them and looked at them closely.

"I've never seen them before," he said confidently and gave them back to me.

"Then who brought them?"

"I didn't. I've done my bit."

"What was your bit?"

He sighed deeply and moistened his lips.

"To show you that you aren't safe."

He walked around me and left without closing the door. I sat on the bed, confused. I suddenly realized how much Gregorio had loved me, and how much I still loved him. Shit, who was the King Midas of destruction now?

I spent the rest of the night sitting on the bed, with the door open, without moving, thinking of the festering air of a distant African savannah.

• • •

I DIDN'T GO BACK HOME; I stayed to live at the motel. I pay for the room and support myself by working for Camariña. I'm in charge of accounting and I supervise the administration of the rooms. I even made some architectural improvements. The motel looks more modern, more functional, and the clientele has definitely increased. Not much, but it has.

Camariña trusts me completely and only comes to the motel every third day, in the evenings. My accounting is neat and clear, with a detailed balance of income and expenditures. I even report how much we spend on soap a day. He says that if I keep it up, he's going to make me a partner.

In my room I have a TV, a shelf with books, a sound system, and a phone connected to Camariña's private line. I bought a copy of *Músico de Cortesanas,* which I always keep on the night-stand. I still use it as my personal *I Ching* and it's almost never wrong.

My relationship with my parents changed for the better once I stopped living at home, especially with my mother. We have lunch together every Saturday. My father still complains about the noise made by the young girl next door; Luis still skips from one lackluster girlfriend to the next, and my mother still makes chicken sandwiches with onions. She's gone back to work. Now she's the coordinator of citizen action in the Benito Juárez dis-trict. She's no longer overwhelmed by not being at home, and she no longer feels guilty.

MARGARITA LIED. Neither Joaquín nor her parents found out about our relationship. She told me that, she confessed, to protect herself. She was also afraid of me. I thought she was being unfair. We'd been friends, accomplices, confidants. She knew so much about me that it would've been difficult to hurt her. And despite that, I did.

I made love to her three more times: once at her house, another time in 803, and the last in the middle of the street in the early morning. All three times were rushed. She did it with a certain rage and fear. I did it with abandon, indifferently, almost just because I could. Since then we've grown distant and our contact has been reduced to a sporadic phone call. I know she has a boyfriend she doesn't love, to whom she might get married.

ACCORDING TO MANRIQUE, Jacinto went back to the mental hospital. He suffers from severe manic depression. To avoid trouble with him, his stepfather (the minister of the interior) grants him his every whim, one of which was to ask for my release from custody. But with the slightest excuse, he locks him up again. Jacinto is back in the world of Prozac, Tegretol, and ridiculous blue gowns.

TANIA DISAPPEARED. It's been more than a year and I haven't heard from her. Her parents have combed through morgues, hospitals, and jails. They travel anguished from one city to the next following up false leads. There's always someone who is sure they've seen her somewhere or other. And there they go to look for her, only to return a few days later, disappointed.

I know Tania is okay, that she thinks about me, that she still loves me. Luis tells me that sometimes, in the middle of the night, the phone rings at home. There's no voice, just breath, and then they hang up. It's her, I'm sure of it.

I haven't been able to forget her. I miss her every night. I sleep naked with the hope that one day she'll cross the room's threshold and come lie down next to me. Because I can't stop loving her. I've tried and I can't do it. I've made love to eight or ten more women, and every time I penetrate I remember Tania's warm belly on me and I close my eyes and think of her.

I'VE BEEN BACK TO THE ZOO. I always head straight to the jaguar pit. I watch the solitary female for hours. Sometimes I can hear a soft purr while she sleeps. It is a sad, ancient purr. I imagine that animals dream and that she dreams of the lost male, with rows of students crowding to watch her, the noise of airplanes overhead.

The female dreams and purrs.

THE LAST MESSAGE I got from Gregorio consisted of an envelope with three earwigs in it and a white, bloodspattered card with the phrase: "The night buffalo dreams of us." I never found out who sent it.

ONCE I WENT TO SEE A MOVIE. It was about two brothers who were very rebellious in their youth. When they grew up, one became a cop, the other a criminal. The cop chose a tranquil, family life, the crook a dark, nomadic one.

One afternoon, in a bar, the crook accuses his brother of having lost his fire, that he's been dominated and humiliated, that he's turned into a caricature of himself. He urges him to recover his fire, to abandon this routine of the boring, responsible man. The cop doesn't answer. He just breaks a bottle on the bar and cuts one of his forearms with the broken glass. "Hell burns on the inside," he tells him, dripping blood. The brother looks at him amazed. Calmly, the cop offers him the bloody glass. His brother doesn't take it and runs away.

THERE ARE MANY NIGHTS I wake up with the blue breath of the night buffalo on my neck. It's death brushing against me, I know it. It's the temptation to put a bullet through my forehead, to end it all. It's the fire that burns me on the inside.

It's death, I know it.